What Remains of Her

a novel

Nicole Palermo

This is a work of fiction. Names, characters, places, and events are either the product of the author's imagination or used fictitiously. Any resemblance to actual persons, living or dead, or actual events is purely coincidental.

Published by Midnight Ocean Press

ISBN 979-8-9946708-1-1

Cover design by Clint English
clintenglish.com

Edited by Hanna Elizabeth

Printed in the United States of America and other countries

Content Note

This novel is set in the 1970s and depicts institutional abuse, including period-accurate homophobic language used by characters to dehumanize others. This language is not endorsed by the author and is included to reflect the historical reality and power structures of the setting.

For those who remain

especially those who have been told they shouldn't

One

Ravensbrook Sanitarium, 1970s

There's something I'm supposed to remember.

I'm sure I knew it once. It's long gone now.

I look out the dirty, grime-streaked window. The sky is gray, and you can feel the moisture outside as though you're part of the mist.

Even inside, the world around me is dense and foggy.

I know there are others, but their lines are blurred and distant regardless of proximity.

I look down at my lunch. The tray is still full.

Didn't I eat? I thought I had.

I pick up a slimy peach, and it slides off the fork and back onto the tray.

I don't think I'm very hungry.

"Nadia, you need to eat your lunch," says one of the nurses, looking at my untouched tray. She looks grim, her mouth a straight line. It's like a child drew it in pencil and forgot her lips. Her skin is almost gray. It clashes against the bright white of her uniform.

"I'm not very hungry," I tell her, looking back out the window. It feels brighter out there, despite the gloom.

She sighs heavily. "You know you need to eat some of it. Your meds may suppress your appetite, but we can't have you starving to death." She puts her clipboard down on the table next to me and picks up my fork. She stabs a very overcooked slab of what might be meat and shoves it into my mouth.

I chew obediently. It's not a good idea to argue. Bad things happen when you don't do what you're told. Resisting any part of your treatment plan is grounds for the seclusion room. I don't want to go back there.

She stabs another piece with the fork and tells me to eat it.

When I do, she grabs her clipboard and moves on to the next patient.

I eat a little more on my own. Enough that she won't come back.

There's a distinct smell to the dining hall, like junior high cafeteria meets nursing home. Sweat, body odor, cigarette smoke, and cheap meat permeate the area. It's not a pleasant place to be, but if I'm being honest, there isn't a pleasant room in this facility.

The nurse stops by my table again, glancing at my tray to ensure I made an attempt to eat. She nods, seemingly satisfied, and makes a note in my chart before moving on.

I long ago lost track of what day it is, but after lunch, we meet with the doctors in our rooms during rounds.

At least, I think that's what happens after lunch.

I don't correctly remember a lot of the time anymore. Much of my life prior to Ravensbrook Institute has been lost, really.

Occasionally, there are flashes of people or a brief memory that appears, but then my meds kick in, and they're lost again.

I typically spend my days, well, dazed, for lack of a better term. I do my best to play nice and not anger anyone. I've learned it's not a good idea to argue.

I glance around, looking for the others with blurry outlines. Someone I know is sitting two tables over. Betty, I think her name is. Or is it Paula? She sees me looking and gets up, then shuffles over to my table.

"Hey," she says, sliding into the chair across from me. "Did you know this used to be a tuberculosis clinic when it was built? One of those 'wellness retreats' for rich people." She moves her head to look directly into my eyes, to see if I'm paying attention. She's high-strung, and she taps her nails on the table.

"Oh?" I try to sound attentive, but I don't care.

"Yeah, Ravensbrook was built in the 1890s or something. Know how many people it's supposed to hold?" She looks like the cat who ate the canary, like she's holding back a secret she thinks I just can't wait to hear.

"How many?" I wish she'd go away. My head is starting to hurt.

"Just a hundred," she says, frowning. "There's almost four hundred now. I overheard two of the nurses talking." She picks at a cuticle.

"Oh. Wow." I want to go back to my room. The lights here are too bright, and Betty/Paula's voice is making my headache worse.

"Can you believe that? In eighty years, it went from a place for rich people to a loony bin where they drug us to keep us in line. One of these days I'm going to get out of here, I really am." She's agitated now.

I think the nurses may need to up her dosage.

She's quiet for a moment, then blurts out, "Do you hear the screams at night?" She looks at me, wide-eyed.

I think this is what she really wanted to ask me. The information about the building was a segue.

"Sometimes," I say truthfully. Occasionally, my meds start to wear off late into the night, and I lie in bed awake.

I hear the screams, even though I try not to.

Before Betty/Paula can ask another question, a nurse taps my tray and tells me it's time to go back to my room. I stand up slowly. "Bye… Betty," I guess. She doesn't correct me, so either I got it right, or she doesn't care.

The world spins for a moment when I stand. Just as it's starting to settle, I feel another tap, this time on my shoulder.

"Get going, Moren, we don't have all day." I think Moren is my last name; they sometimes use it instead of Nadia.

I'll forget it again by tomorrow.

I shuffle down the long, wide hallway. The smell of alcohol and ammonia wafts through the open space. It must have been a beautiful building eighty years ago, but now it's a sad, crumbling remnant of an institution. All of the old solariums and extra hallways were turned into wards long ago. The sunlight that healed the soul is now replaced by the hum of overhead fluorescents, and the windows are so old and bloated they no longer open.

Rooms that used to house two residents now accommodate up to six. Metal bed frames are lined up side by side, so you have to climb into bed from the bottom. Cots are so thin that the springs poke you in the back at night. There's a single bureau with a drawer for each patient.

I take a left and continue shuffling back toward my room. I pass by a procedure room where shock therapy is done. The room seems slightly familiar, and I think I may have been in there before, but I don't have specific memories of being shocked. Other things happen in there too, but I've been lucky to avoid finding out what those are.

I shudder slightly, thinking about the screams.

I approach my room, number 108. I'm lucky to only have three roommates. I used to have four, but one went for treatment one day and never came back.

They haven't replaced her.

As I open the door, the Judys look up from their cots.

Mary doesn't bother. She's so heavily medicated that she's staring into space.

Doctor Herbert is already here, going through Judy 1's file with her. Judy must have been a popular name in the 40s.

"Yes, Judith, there's a new medicine we're going to try out because of your recent reactions to the Thorazine. Haldol is a newer drug, and we're going to see how well you take to it." He scribbles in Judy 1's chart, and she nods complacently.

A nurse hands her a paper cup with pills in it. She throws them back and swallows them with a swig of water, then sticks out her tongue. The nurse checks her mouth to confirm it's empty.

Dr. Herbert looks over at the door. "Ah, Nadia. Thanks for showing up before rounds are over," sounding slightly irritated, he shifts to the other foot impatiently.

I have to remind myself not to stare at the upside-down heart-shaped birthmark that sits just under his left eye. It can be mesmerizing.

"Sorry, Doctor Herbert," I say quietly as I shuffle over to my bed and sit down. I try not to look up at him. He's in his early fifties with gray hair that used to be dark. He has a kind face, but it's an illusion.

He picks up my chart and briefly rifles through it, then speaks to the nurse. He doesn't look at me. "Okay. Nadia Moren. Female. Thirty-four years old. Manic-depressive psychosis resulting in acute agitation. Delusional behavior when not well-medicated. Currently managed with Thorazine and Lithium. Seems like we'll keep her at the current dosage. Handled electroshock therapy well, no additional treatments needed at this time." He sticks his pen behind his ear and turns toward the door.

The nurse hands me my paper cup.

"Um, Doctor Herbert?" I say shyly, half hoping he doesn't hear me. I know the staff doesn't like to be bothered by patients.

He turns back. "Yes?" He looks surprised that I spoke.

"Sorry to bother you. Do… do you know where I came from?" It's a question that has been bothering me lately. Or at least, it's bothering me right now. I guess I can't recall if it's been on my mind longer.

He stares at me for a moment, then looks down at my chart. He riffles through the pages before landing on the one with helpful information. He looks back up. "You came from living with family. Your psychosis became burdensome, and they had you committed." His voice has lost its typical edge; I can almost hear a hint of pity.

"Oh, okay. Thank you."

He takes his leave of the room.

I take my paper cup of pills with a swig of water, and the nurse hurries off behind him after checking my mouth.

I'm not sure what made me ask. I usually try not to bother anyone. Attracting negative attention is a bad idea here.

"This room smells like piss," Judy 2 says to nobody in particular. She's smoking a cigarette, and her dark hair flops across her forehead as if its goal is to irritate her. "Did one of you piss yourselves again?" She's frequently agitated. I don't know what's wrong with her, but she ends up in the seclusion room a lot, and it doesn't seem to help.

"I don't smell anything," Judy 1 says, sounding slightly offended. Judy 1 used to be pretty, you can tell. I can almost picture her with her short blonde hair washed and styled, in a pair of Jackie O sunglasses, riding down the boulevard in her man's convertible. Not anymore.

Now she's as drab as the rest of us.

Judy 2's face darkens, like she might pick a fight with Judy 1.

I don't want the orderlies coming in here; it means bad news for all of us. "It's quiet hour!" I whisper-yell at the two of them. "Shut your traps."

Judy 2 lies down on her bed, still looking angry, but she's thankfully quiet. Tendrils of smoke curl off the end of her cigarette as she stares at the ceiling, subdued for now.

I'm not sure how she sneaks the matches in, but somehow she always has some.

I lie down and close my eyes, just to have something to do. A while later, I open them. I may have dozed off for a bit, but everything is so fuzzy it's always hard to tell.

Mary is still sitting and dissociating. The Judys are lying on their beds, facing each other, having a conversation in whispers.

An orderly opens the door, and the Judys and I sit up.

The orderlies are the staff you want to see the least around here. They're the bulldogs. The ones called in when control or damage is required.

Whichever will get the job done.

"Judy Dean, visitor. The rest of you, activities room." He turns and closes the door again. The three of us all let out our breath.

I hadn't realized I was holding mine.

I get up and walk over to Mary's cot. Shaking her gently, I say, "Mary, activity time."

Her eyes slowly come into focus, and she looks at me. "What?"

"Quiet time is over; we have to go to the activity room." I try to be gentle with her. She seems fragile.

"Oh. Okay. Thanks." She slowly gets up from her cot and heads toward the door.

I wonder where she goes when she dissociates, and if it's better or worse than being here.

I start my own shuffle down the hall to the 'activity' room. It's one of the better rooms in this place. You can put together puzzles that are all missing a half dozen pieces, read the same years-old magazines that have sat there forever, or play solitaire. You can also pull up a chair and watch sitcom reruns. We're discouraged from socializing, though the nurses will let it slide if you're quiet.

I sit at an empty table that has a partially finished puzzle waiting. Picking up a piece, I turn it over in my fingers. It feels strange, almost stale. I look down at the completed part of the picture. It looks like a car's front bumper and tire. I pick up the box to see what the full image is supposed to be. It's a dog standing upright, filling the gas tank.

It's unsettling.

I put the box back down and get up. I don't feel like doing a puzzle now.

Picking up a magazine, I sit at another table. After flipping a few pages, I realize I haven't actually read a word.

I think I feel… different right now. Something is off. I'm restless.

I look up to see if anyone I know is around. The light from the TV distorts people's faces, making it difficult to tell whether they're familiar.

I spot Judy 1 sitting near me, watching TV. She has an empty seat next to her. I get up. Maybe I'll go sit with her and watch *Bewitched.*

Something feels wrong.

Unexpectedly, there's a hand on my shoulder. It's one of the nurses, the nicer one. She has dark, curly hair. I can see her dainty cross necklace.

What's her name? Nurse Cross? No, that's not right. Delaney, I think it is.

"Nadia, hon, where are you going?" She has a concerned look on her face.

"Oh, hi, Nurse… Delaney." I hope I got her name right. "I was just going to sit next to Judy and watch TV." I take a step in that direction, and she stops me.

"Nadia, are you okay? You seem off. Jumpy. Did something happen?" She guides me back down into the chair I was just sitting in. "Did you need an extra dose today?" She searches my face for signs that I'm not medicated enough.

I don't want extra meds. "No, I'm just fine," I say, trying to sound as cheerful as I can in a place where there isn't any cheer to be found.

Picking the magazine back up, I comment on a headline. "Did you see these pictures of Karen Carpenter? I guess the residents here aren't the only ones with fragile health." I smile widely up at Nurse Delaney, hoping that I was able to pull off a believable act. Extra meds will turn me into a vegetable, and I definitely don't want that.

She smiles at me. "Okay, hon. As long as you aren't feeling agitated. I'll leave you to your magazine." She moves on to check on the next patient.

I'm relieved. Even the 'nice' nurses are happy to overmedicate you to keep you from becoming an inconvenience.

I'm about to go back to pretending to read my magazine when I feel a shift in energy.

Someone is standing at my side. My breath catches.

It's the little girl in the green dress.

Two

"You're forgetting again," she tells me. Her voice has the soft lilt of childhood innocence. It doesn't sound like an accusation; it's almost conversational.

"I can't remember; I've told you that," I say out loud. Too loud.

Nurse Delaney looks back at me. "Everything okay over there?" She tilts her head as she studies me from across the room.

I brighten and say, "Yes, just fine, thanks!" Turning away, I put my head in my hands and remind myself that I can't talk to the little girl out loud.

She isn't real. I know that for sure. This facility is for adults only. There's never been a child here, at least in my time. My brain manifests this child when my meds are wearing off too early. She's a trick my mind likes to play. Even in my medicated state, I'm aware of this.

Nobody else sees her, and I don't believe in ghosts. "Why are you here?" I whisper to her under my breath.

She looks at me, eyes wide. "I'm here to remind you. You know that." She smiles and sways slightly, side to side, in her pretty green dress. This is what she wears most of the time. The green velvet dress brings out the green in her eyes, and her hair bow is the same material. She's about six years old, and her blonde hair is plaited down her back. She twirls once so I can see her skirt billow outward with her movements.

"You need to go away, you're going to get me in trouble," I tell her, agitated now. I'm trying to stay quiet, but others sitting near me begin to look up. They're wondering who I'm talking to.

"I can't go away until you remember. It's important." She smiles at me sweetly, almost adoringly.

I stand up and bring my hands down on the table loudly, eyes squeezed shut. "GO AWAY! I can't remember!"

Immediately realizing my mistake, I open my eyes and see two orderlies walking toward me.

"NO!" I yell at them. "Leave me alone! I'm fine! I'M FINE!!" I try to sit down, but they each take one of my arms and drag me out into the hallway.

I'm kicking and trying to get away, but one of the nurses injects me with something. I go limp within thirty seconds, and the orderlies half-carry me to a seclusion room.

I'm too medicated to fight back or object.

I'm not sure if I sleep, but I come to at some point, my mouth dry and tasting metallic. There's a tray of cold dinner mush on the floor near the door. The little girl is nowhere to be found.

She tricked me into more meds and seclusion. If I weren't so hazy, I'd be mad. I hope they don't up my dosage now because of my outburst.

What was it she said? *You're forgetting again.* Of course, I'm forgetting.

I remember very little of my life outside of Ravensbrook. I don't know how I'd ever remember, even with help.

And there is nobody here to help me.

I get up off the floor and slowly start to pace back and forth.

It's more of a steady shuffle.

Quietly, of course. I don't want to seem agitated again.

The room is only six by eight feet; the walls lightly padded. There's a single cot mattress, and nothing else. A drain in the floor that smells faintly of ammonia. There's nowhere to relieve yourself.

You can figure out how that goes.

I replay in my mind the interaction with the little girl. It's odd. She's the one thing I never seem to forget.

When she appears in my room, the Judys and Mary don't care if I talk to her as long as I'm quiet. It's almost always an issue if she appears anywhere in public, because just knowing that she can upset me, upsets me.

I don't know what she wants. Only that she got me thrown into seclusion and over-medicated. My head hurts, and the world around me feels extra foggy.

I lie on the floor and stare into the drain. It's just a circular hole with piping that goes directly down into some place unknown to me.

I roll onto my back. It hurts, lying on the floor, my backbone pressed against the concrete. Somehow it feels right.

I realize I need to use the facilities, but I'll hold it. I don't want to knock on the door for fear of seeming agitated, and I certainly don't want to drop my pants and piss into the hole that goes to God knows where.

I stand up and shuffle some more, wondering how much time has gone by. The door opens, and an orderly pops his head in, but just to grab my tray. He doesn't look at or speak to me. It doesn't bother him that I didn't eat.

"Excuse me?" I say, but he's gone again before I have time to tell him I need the bathroom.

I alternate between pacing and lying on the floor for what feels like hours, until I can't hold it anymore.

I pull my pants down and hover above the drain. Just as the urine starts to flow, the door opens, and Doctor Herbert enters.

He's looking down at my chart, but as he's about to speak, he looks up to see me squatting over the drain. It's still coming; I really had to go.

"I'm sorry," I tell him. "I couldn't hold it anymore." I imagine my cheeks must be flushed, but I can't feel them.

He turns and faces the door, waiting until he hears me finish and pull my pants back up. When he turns back around, I'm sitting cross-legged on the mattress. I don't look at him.

He ignores the uncomfortable situation completely. "Nadia, can you tell me what happened today?" He's looking at my chart; he doesn't want to make eye contact either.

"I don't know. I just felt a little off this afternoon. I'm sorry." I won't tell him about the little girl. Even though everyone already knows I'm crazy, and I probably *should* say something, I don't want them to medicate her away.

He sighs heavily. "It's been a while since we've had to adjust your meds. Did something set you off today?" He looks at me over the paperwork.

I still don't make eye contact. "Well, Judy 2 seemed agitated earlier. I think maybe it rubbed off on me." I don't want to throw Judy 2 under the bus, but I'm fighting for my own sanity. "I'm sorry, it won't happen again. I think my meds are the right dose."

Dr. Herbert is still looking at me, as if he's trying to read through my illness to see the truth. He sighs again and takes off his glasses, pinching the bridge of his nose as if to ward off a headache. "Nadia, I need you to be honest with me. It's important for your treatment." He stares at me until I look up at him.

"Honestly, Dr. Herbert. Normally, I feel even keeled on my meds. Today was a one-off, I promise." I hope I'm telling the truth for my own sake.

He nods, looking satisfied. Making a note in my chart, he says, "Okay, we'll give it a few days to make sure that the dosage is still right. Any more outbursts, though, and we'll have to up your meds." He walks over and knocks on the door. An orderly opens it, and he instructs them to return me to room 108.

We pass a window on the walk back, and it's very dark outside. "What time is it?" I ask the orderly.

"Shut up," he snarls at me. He unlocks the door to my room and pushes me inside, locking it behind me.

Inside, it's pitch black. I assume that everyone else is asleep because there's no noise. I feel my way over to my bedframe, and climb in. Lying in the near-total darkness, I can faintly hear someone snoring. Another rolls over, and her cot creaks. I don't know if Mary is sleeping, but the thought of her sitting up, dissociating in the dark, is disconcerting.

I try to run through today in my head, try to remember everything that happened. What did I have for breakfast? Not sure. Lunch? Nope. I didn't eat dinner. I only remember the seclusion room and the little girl.

Maybe she's right. I'm just not trying hard enough to remember. I know there's something I'm forgetting, something important.

I lie in the dark, listening. The room smells of sweat and old cigarette smoke.

As I'm starting to drift off to sleep, I hear it.

The screams.

Shrieks of terror floating into my room.

I fall asleep to the sound of a metal gurney being pushed down the hall, wheels squeaking, while its occupant moans in pain.

Three

The sun streaks through the dirty windows as I wake to an orderly turning on the bright overhead lights.

He yells, "Wake up! Medicine rounds!"

The four of us sit up slowly in bed, waiting for the nurses to come in with our pills.

The little girl is sitting cross-legged on the floor by my bed, but she doesn't speak.

I never got my nighttime meds yesterday, so it makes sense that she's here. The delicate fabric of her dress glistens in the dirty sunlight.

The nurse comes in, and the girl stands, still staring at me. "Moren, Thorazine." The nurse hands me the paper cup. I throw the pills back with water, and the girl shakes her head. She looks sad for a few moments, then slowly fades away.

I'm relieved that she's gone, but I feel a pang of sadness too.

As the meds kick in and I'm drawn away from everything that happened yesterday, I realize I'm supposed to try and remember. I need to figure out a way to try. It slips away from me as I'm thinking about it, and all I can think about is that it's cold in my room and the floor is shadowy.

A short time later, we're called for breakfast. Powdered eggs, fatty bacon, and dry toast. I eat enough that the nurses leave me alone. As I'm walking back from breakfast to my room, I see a pen lying on the floor.

I stop.

It's a strange thing to see just lying there. Everything in this facility is very locked down, and things don't slip through the cracks. I stare at it, thinking.

My pulse quickens. This feels strange because I normally feel nothing on my meds.

I'm still staring at it when Nurse Delaney walks up behind me.

"You okay, Nadia?" She looks down and sees the pen. "Oh my," she says, swooping down to pick it up. "We don't want anyone getting hurt. Good catch, Moren." She gives me a gentle push on the small of my back, and I continue walking to 108.

Sitting in my room, the pen is on my mind. I obviously know what a pen is for. But finding one just lying on the floor feels significant in a way I can't make myself comprehend.

My morning is a haze, and I focus on the grimy window and the light filtering through it. For a while, I watch Mary, watching nothing.

The pen continues to enter my thoughts, on and off. I can't figure out why it matters, but I feel like it does.

It has to. It isn't gone yet.

Lunch goes by in a blurry fog. I spend quiet time staring at the ceiling, listening to the Judys argue quietly. Mary says nothing.

The door opens, and an orderly yells out, "Activities room! Nadia Moren, visitor!"

I'm surprised, or as surprised as I can be in my semi-lucid state.

Do I normally have visitors?

I shuffle down the hall, wandering. I'm not sure where I'm supposed to go to see a visitor.

An orderly stops me, "Why aren't you in the activities room?" He looks angry that he has to stop what he's doing.

"They said I have a visitor, but I'm not sure where to go." I look at him and wait docilely for an answer.

He sighs, then grabs my arm and pulls me into an area I don't recognize.

Do I? Maybe I've been here before.

The room looks vaguely familiar. There are several small areas set up with comfortable-looking armchairs and tables. Patients sit across from their visitors and talk quietly. Some are crying.

Looking around, I spot a single man with nobody sitting across from him. He's in his late thirties, with dark hair that borders on messy, and dark eyes. His stubble is a few days old. There's a brooding look to him, and eyebrows that belong on a movie poster. He looks up from twiddling his fingers and sees me.

He stands up. "Nadia!" he says, striding toward me and giving me a hug. His face looks sorrowful.

He leads me back to the armchair across from him and then sits again. He speaks quietly. "Nadia, how are you?" His perfect brows furrow, and there's no hint of a smile.

I smile politely. "I'm fine. How are you?" He looks familiar, but I can't place him. It probably doesn't help that he's blurry from my afternoon meds.

My attention shifts to the shades of green in the armchair I'm sitting in. The small stripes of forest, lime, and avocado are enchanting.

I run my fingers over them. They're soft to the touch.

"It smells nice in here," I say conversationally.

It does. It smells sort of like vanilla. It's a nice change from the smells in the rest of the place.

I should be polite to my guest, even if I don't know him. He seems to know me. I smile at him.

He looks genuinely taken aback. "Fine? You don't look fine." He sits back in his own chair and folds his arms. "What the hell are they doing to you here?"

I look back up at him. "They're taking care of me. I'm following my treatment plan." I gaze into his eyes and realize they're rimmed with a lighter gold color than the dark centers. I wonder who this man is, and how he knows me.

He looks horrified. "Nadia, are you okay?" He looks over toward the chaperones. There are two orderlies and a nurse about ten feet away. "You seem so different. Coming here was supposed to be for the best. I'm starting to doubt that's true." He shifts in his chair, uncomfortable despite the cushiness.

I've been staring at the pretty flowered wallpaper, wondering what it feels like. "I'm fine," I repeat. I decide I should probably know who this man is. "Do you mind if I ask, how do I know you?"

The man goes completely rigid. "Nadia, are you saying you don't remember me?" His voice hits an alarming pitch.

I look down. I hadn't expected him to be so offended. I don't remember anything; it isn't personal. "I… You look familiar, but I don't know you."

The man puts his head in his hands. His face is drawn, eyes wide. "I can't believe this." He gets up from the table and storms up to the nurse.

I can hear him. They aren't far.

"She doesn't even remember me. I'm her BROTHER! How can this happen? She's been here two months! Last month, she seemed tired, but at least she knew who I was. What is going on in this facility?" His voice is raised, and the other patients and visitors are now looking up to see what the yelling is about.

The nurse calms him. "I'm sorry that you had to see her this way. It's typical at this point for her memory to be foggy. It usually passes by the time she's adjusted to her meds. It's one of the reasons we discourage visitors for the first three months of treatment. You're welcome to stay and visit with her, but you need to stay calm. Being angry will only agitate her and make the rest of her day harder. Try to have a pleasant visit with your sister and know that this stage will pass." She puts a hand on his shoulder.

So, he's my brother. It makes sense that he looks familiar.

He sits back down and immediately puts his head in his hands again. "I am so sorry, Nadia." He looks up at me, and even in my state, I can read the sorrow on his face. He reaches out and takes my hands. "I didn't know it would be like this. I would never have let them put you here if I had."

"Who?" I ask. I don't know why it occurred to me.

"Who, what?" he returns.

"Who 'put me here'?"

He tilts his head slightly to the side. "I cannot believe you can't remember anything. Mom and Dad, Nadia." His voice has taken on a disbelieving quality.

"Oh, right." I don't remember them at all. Then something else occurs to me. "Sorry, I know my forgetting bothers you, but what's your name?" I think knowing may help me connect some of the pieces.

"God, you don't even remember my name." His eyes fill.

"It's okay. You don't have to tell me." I don't want to upset him more.

I shouldn't have asked.

"Vic. My name is Vic." He squeezes my hand.

It feels nice.

"When I get home, I'm going to talk to Mom and Dad. We can't leave you here. I didn't like this idea to begin with, and now I'm certain I was right." He's flushed now.

I don't have a memory of being put here or anything before that.

I only remember the little girl and the pen.

"Vic," I whisper very quietly. "Do you have a pen?"

He looks at me strangely, then searches the pockets of his jeans.

I look over at the orderlies and the nurse, but they're busy flirting.

Vic comes up empty. Then I see a lightbulb go off in his head, and he tries his back pocket. He finds what he's looking for. Sensing that this is against the rules, he slides it under his hand, then rests it back over mine.

I bend down and slide the pen into my slipper. I still don't know why I need it, but I know I do.

I look up again at Vic. "Can you bring another one the next time you visit?"

He smiles sadly. "I'm so glad you're still in there somewhere, Nadia."

Four

There's still an hour left of activity time. I can feel the pen pressing against the top of my foot and my toes.

Vic promised to come back next week. He said he's going to visit weekly until he can convince Mom and Dad to release me and bring me home. He seems to genuinely care about me.

I'm glad. It's nice to know someone does.

I'm sitting at a table, alone, with magazines spread around me. I'm not agitated today. The little girl is nowhere to be seen. Reruns of *I Dream of Jeannie* are playing on the TV. I never liked that show.

I remember not liking that show. That's new.

Maybe my visit with Vic knocked loose a few memories? It's sad, though. After tonight's dose of meds, I won't remember Vic again. I won't remember that I don't like *I Dream of Jeannie.*

I pick up another magazine, pretending to read. A small card falls out. It's the insert you mail in to subscribe. I pick it up and look at it. Name, Address, Phone Number. You have to fill it out for the magazine to be delivered to you.

You have to fill it out.

In pen.

A lightbulb flickers briefly in my brain, and I pick up the small card. I tuck it into the waistband of my pants.

I know I need to act before I forget.

I get up and walk over to one of the nurses. She turns. It's Nurse Delaney.

"Excuse me? Nurse Delaney?" I say politely.

"Yes, hon?" She's distracted. Another patient is restless, and she's paying close attention.

"Can I use the bathroom?" I stand with my hands at my side, awaiting her reply.

"Um, yes, go right ahead. Thanks for letting me know." She doesn't look up again.

There's a bathroom attached to the activity room, but you have to let the nurses know you're using it. They like to make sure they know where everyone is at all times. As I'm walking over, an orderly stops me.

"Where are you going?" He's irritated. They're always irritated.

"Bathroom. Nurse Delaney said it was okay."

He calls to her, "Delaney! This one okay?" while he points to me.

She gives him a thumbs-up. He lets go and walks off without wasting another second on me.

I go into the bathroom and close the door. My heart is beating faster than normal. I take the card out of my waistband and the pen out of my shoe. My hands are trembling, despite my meds. I click the pen once and start to fill out the card.

Nadia Moran
4810 Pebble Drive
South Barrow NJ
201-258-6174

I stare at the card in my hand, shocked.

Did this just happen? I started to write my name, and muscle memory did the rest.

I have a brief flicker of an image: a small house on the shore. Yellow, with periwinkle blue shutters.

The other side of the card is blank except for the magazine's return address. I write:

Yellow house – blue shutters.

Then I add:

Little girl – green dress
Vic – Brother

I realize I've been in here too long. I put the card back in my waistband and the pen back in my shoe.

As I exit, Nurse Delaney is waiting for me. "Everything okay, Moren?"

"Yes, Nurse Delaney. I'm fine. I had a little bit of an upset stomach, but I'm good now." I hold my stomach and smile a lopsided smile at her, doing my best impression of a good patient.

The truth is, the rush of realizing I know my name and address cut through the drugs, and I'm on a different kind of high right now. I understand very clearly how I need to proceed. My memory may be cloudy, but it isn't actually gone.

Nurse Delaney looks at me closely, then decides I'm telling the truth. "Glad you're feeling better. Activity time is just about over." She walks back to check on her other patient, who is now very sedated.

At dinner, I sit with the Judys. Mary is here too, but only physically. Betty sees me and comes over to sit with us.

The fog has settled back in. My mental clarity from an hour ago is gone, but the feeling hasn't abandoned me. I still know there's something I'm supposed to be doing.

The ladies are all mumbling quietly about the terrible food. They aren't wrong. I'm staring into the mush on my plate when I remember I'm supposed to be doing something.

It had to do with the pen.

What was it?

I can't remember. I'm frustrated.

I turn to Betty. "Do you remember before you were here?"

She looks at me, shocked.

I don't talk much. I usually don't have anything to say.

Betty recovers and leans forward; her long black hair hangs like a curtain. She's using it as a shield from the nurses. "Usually I do," she whispers. "I used to be a bartender. I made the mistake of getting married and knocked up. I was depressed when my kid was born. They threw me in here and said I had a 'breakdown.' Like it isn't normal to cry when your whole life changes." She clenches her fists on the tabletop.

I wish I hadn't asked.

I nod, feeling sorry for her. "I'm sorry, Betty. That's tough."

"I'm going to get out of here, though." She seems angry. Her face has gone an unhealthy shade of red. "Any day now. They're going to let me out, and I'll see my baby again." Tears start to silently run down her face.

I made a mistake asking. Our table is going to get attention we don't need.

"I remember." The voice comes out of Mary, and I turn and stare at her. She's younger than the rest of us. Early twenties and very pretty. "I won't let myself forget." She looks at me. Her light brown hair brushes her shoulders as she turns her head slightly to make eye contact.

Betty's crying tapers off, and she wipes her face with a napkin. She takes a few deep breaths and listens.

Mary speaks again. "My family threw me in here for being 'promiscuous.' They wanted to marry me off, and I said, 'Hell, no.' They didn't like that. Thought I was a liability, that I was going to come home pregnant. I was studying science in college. I know what places like this do to girls like me." She shudders, and I can see her hands shaking. "I just try to stay quiet and mind my business. It's better than a chemical lobotomy." She looks at me again. "But I remember everything. I won't let myself forget."

As quickly as the words came out of her mouth, it was like she was gone again. Back into the world she lives in behind her own eyes. It must be better there.

The four of us look at each other quietly. We're probably all wondering the same thing.

Did that really happen?

Did we imagine it?

"I don't really remember," I tell them. "I want to, but I don't. My brother came to visit me today, and I didn't know who he was. Didn't even know his name. He said he's going to talk to Mom and Dad about taking me home again."

Judy 2 snorts. "Don't count on it." Her face is twisted like something smells bad. "People don't leave here unless it's in a body bag."

Betty lets out a loud sob, and Judy 2 realizes her mistake, too late.

"Sorry, Betty. I didn't mean that, honest. I'm sure your situation is different!" But it doesn't help.

Betty dissolves into tears, sobbing loudly.

A nurse rushes over and stands Betty up. "What on earth happened over here?" She looks at all the faces at the table. We all do our best to look dull. Like we don't know why she's crying. Nobody answers.

The nurse walks Betty away, and there's a collective sigh of relief.

Judy 2 says, "That was close."

"Yeah, well, you could lighten up a little." Judy 1's face is red, and her tone is blistering. "You don't need to be such a hag all the time."

Judy 2's mouth hangs open, as if Judy 1 just slapped her.

Judy 1 gets up from the table and moves to an empty one halfway across the room. She sits with her back to us.

Message received.

After dinner, we're allowed more TV time. I sit near the magazines and pretend to read them. They feel familiar in my hand, and I know I'm supposed to remember something. I shift my foot in my slipper, and it bumps against the pen.

Recognition hits, and it reminds me of my task. When the nurses aren't looking, I slip two more cards into my waistband. That way, I won't have to do it again for a while. The riskiest part is being caught stealing the cards.

I look over, and the Judys are sitting next to each other, watching *The Mary Tyler Moore Show*. Their hands hang down between them, and from this angle, it almost looks like they're touching.

I pretend to read for a while longer. I'm actually trying to remember what I should write down tonight. I don't want to forget. I need to start taking notes if I'm ever going to make progress.

At bedtime, the nurses make their rounds with our meds. One hands me my cup, and I throw it back with water, then open my mouth and move my tongue so she can see it's gone. She takes the cup and moves on.

When the nurses leave the room, I take the pill out from between my upper lip and gums and shove it in my pillowcase. It's a small pill, but if they had been looking for it, they would have seen it.

The Judys are on the two beds closest to the door, side by side. Mary is sitting on the far bed, but she isn't looking at me. I lie with my back to the Judys and take the pen out of my shoe. I slip the notecard out of my waistband.

I look up. Mary is still staring straight ahead.

I turn so that I can write with my right hand. I add:

Mary – Promiscuous
Betty – Baby breakdown

I click the pen to close it. Mary is looking at me. She gives me a half-smile, then continues staring straight ahead.

The Judys didn't notice. They're cuddling. That's a dangerous game in a place like this.

I sit back up to store the pen and the card in my pillowcase.

The little girl is sitting at the foot of my bed.

She smiles.

Five

I wake late into the night. Moonlight is shining through our window.

That's not what woke me.

It's the screams.

They're very loud. Not just screams of terror, but of pain. The sound ricochets down the hallway. I get up and look out the small window into the hall.

It's dark. I can't see anything at all.

I try the door. It's locked.

Of course it is. It's always locked.

I feel clearer than I have in a while. I've partially slept off my meds. Avoiding the bedtime meds has me in a spot where I feel sharp for the first time since I can remember.

I look back at the beds. The Judys have fallen asleep, cuddling. Mary is sleeping too. I'm glad she doesn't just stare into the darkness all night.

I go back to my bed and search through the pillowcase.

Pulling out the pen and a new card, I start to draw.

Hair. Eyes. A soft cheekbone. I continue sketching until the portrait is finished. I hold it up in the moonlight.

"It looks just like me," she says. She's sitting on my bed, legs crossed. She's wearing pajamas now.

"It does look just like you," I whisper back to her. I don't want to wake anyone. "Now I'll never forget."

She smiles up at me. "You'll remember. I know you can do it."

I smile back. "Can I ask you something?" My face falls.

"Of course," she says. "What is it?"

"You… aren't real… right? I know you're not, but I need you to tell me." I don't know why, but I feel nervous.

"No, silly. I'm not real. I'm just here to remind you. That's all." She smiles at me again.

I know it's odd, but I'm relieved. I didn't think she was a ghost, but it comforts me to know that she's just a figment of my damaged imagination.

The morning sun streams through the window. I'm awake before the orderly comes in and yells, "Med rounds! Everyone up!"

I sit up slowly, like I always do. I need to act as slow and dull as possible. If I'm found to be avoiding my pills, things can get much worse for me.

The nurses come in and hand out paper cups and pills to everyone.

I throw mine back, but don't get it into my upper lip fast enough.

Shit. I have to swallow it, or I'll be found out. I swallow.

Maybe it will be fine? If I can even cut back to half of the doses I've been taking, is it possible the world will be a little clearer?

An hour later, I'm shuffling out of breakfast.

I know there was something I'm supposed to remember. What was it again? I try to recall, but my brain feels mushy today.

Maybe it was nothing.

Back in room 108, I'm waiting with the Judys and Mary for Doctor Herbert to make his rounds. He comes in, and I try not to look at his heart birthmark.

He deals with the Judys first, then addresses me directly. "Nadia, how have you been feeling the last couple of days?"

I'm caught off guard. Why is he talking to me? Doesn't he usually only talk to the nurse? "I'm fine, thank you," I reply. I'm not sure what information he wants.

He looks at me for a moment. "You've been fine since seclusion the other day? There's nothing in your file noting any added agitation, but I wanted to be sure."

Was I in seclusion? I don't remember that. "Yes, just fine. Thank you."

He nods and turns to the nurse. "Keep her on the fifty milligram Thorazine, three times a day. For now."

The nurse hands me my paper cup, and I take it. I throw back my pill and wash it down with water.

An orderly comes in to escort us to 'occupational therapy.'

We get to the laundry room and are shown how to fold towels and sheets. They don't let us run the washers and dryers.

I know I've done this a few times since being here, though I'm not sure how often we work.

Nurse Delaney is supervising us. She occasionally gets up to check that we're folding correctly. She walks down the aisles of tables, humming a song.

She stops here and there to correct a crease or a fold. Then she continues on, humming all the way. She seems happier than the other nurses here. Maybe this is actually her calling.

Though I can't imagine that dealing with drugged-up loons is anyone's calling.

I'm paired up with Betty. Something about her is different. I briefly wonder what happened. She's slower than usual. Not speaking. Her eyes are directed at something far away, but when I look, there's nothing there. I try to ask, but Nurse Delaney shushes me.

We're not supposed to talk.

We spend two hours folding hot sheets and towels. Next, we're escorted out for a walk around the institute. It's a clear fall day, and it smells like leaves and wet earth. The ground squishes under my feet.

It's strangely pleasant.

The orderlies patrol us, making sure nobody tries to run. It would be interesting to see someone try. They wouldn't get far.

The near-midday sun warms me, just as a breeze cools my face and neck. A strand of hair flies across my face. It's brown and mousy. Drab. It feels like the right color for where my life has brought me.

By the time we get back inside, I'm tired. It's the most activity I've had in as long as I can remember.

Granted, that isn't very long.

We're allowed to go back to our rooms to change.

I walk in just as the Judys are separating. I'm not sure exactly what I walked into, but I know if a nurse or orderly saw it, there would be consequences for them. I shiver at the thought.

Mary is sitting on her bed, looking straight ahead at nothing. She probably didn't see anything, but I know she heard whatever it was. I don't think she'll tell.

I lie on my bed, staring at the ceiling. Something crinkles under my head. Weird. I reach into my pillowcase and find notes that I wrote to myself. I don't remember doing this, but it must be important if I hid it in my pillowcase.

There's a card from a magazine, filled out with my whole name and address. When did I do this? The other side has notes I wrote to myself.

I have a brother? Mary is a slut? Betty is a mom?

I look at the next card, and it's a drawing of the little girl. It looks remarkably like her.

Almost lifelike.

Something strains in my head, something I'm supposed to remember. I can feel it pressing against my brain, screaming to escape. It feels like it's important. I search around in my pillowcase again. There's a pen. I'm hiding a pen, notes, and the drawing.

I take my pillow out of the case and dump it out. A small pill falls out. I pick it up, turn it over in my fingers. It's one of the pills they give me three times a day.

I didn't take one? Why? I could get into so much trouble if they find out.

My foggy brain is trying to solve the puzzle when the door starts to swing open. I quickly throw the pill, pen, and papers back in the case, and start to put my pillow back in. An orderly yells, "Lunch!" without even looking in.

I was lucky. I need to be smarter. I can't be quicker, so I need to use the skills I have.

Despite the brain fog, I can feel the thought trying to press through my skull.

I take the note card out and look at it again. My full name, an address that sounds familiar, and my phone number, all written there nonchalantly as if I was ordering a magazine subscription.

I know I have to go to lunch or they're going to come looking for me, but what do I do with these?

A flicker of recognition starts to form. As I grasp for it, the door opens. I shove the card behind my back quickly.

An orderly pokes his head in. "Moren! Lunch! Now!" he barks at me.

"Sorry, I'm coming." I stand up to show that I'm on my way.

He leaves, keeping the door open behind him.

I hurriedly shove the card back in my pillowcase. The flicker is gone now. I'll have to start over again during quiet hours.

Six

I sit quietly through lunch while the Judys talk.

Betty and Mary are both silent today.

The card, the pen, the pill, all continue to flicker through my thoughts, like a candle desperately trying to stay alight.

I keep coming back to the pill. I must have skipped it intentionally. If I do that again, will I have a better understanding of why I did it last time? If the fog lifts, will it answer some of my questions?

I attempt to eat some of my lunch, and as I shift my attention, I can feel the thoughts and memories of the pill slipping away. I have to continually focus on it to retain it.

There has to be an easier way.

I take a pea off my lunch tray and hold it in my palm. *Pill, Pill, Pill,* I chant to myself, quietly.

I don't even think I said it out loud.

I close my left fist around it and pick up the fork with my right hand. As I eat, I can feel the memory start to slip, but then I squeeze my left fist, and I can feel the "pill" in it. It helps to remind me.

"Everything okay?" Judy 1 asks me. "You have a weird look on your face today. Like something hurts." She seems concerned.

I look up at her. "I'm fine. Just trying to remember something." I squeeze the pea again.

"Okay, as long as you're good. We don't need attention from the nurses." Her concern was not for me, but for all of us.

I get it. I don't want to draw attention either. It's good to know that my determination is written on my face.

As I'm shuffling back to 108, Nurse Delaney stops me.

"Nadia, hon, how are you feeling today?" She puts her hand on my shoulder.

Squeezing the pea, I tell her I'm fine.

"Are you sure? You look pained today. Everything's okay? You don't need another dose?" She has the same look of concern that Judy 1 had earlier.

I definitely don't want another dose. I'm barely holding onto the thought as it is.

I smile at her. "I'm fine. Maybe a little gas from lunch." I've surprised myself. My addled brain hasn't been that quick at thinking up an excuse lately.

I give the pea another squeeze.

She smiles back and gives my shoulder a squeeze. "Okay, hon. Have a relaxing, quiet time, and I'll check in later." She walks away, and I make it back to 108.

I lie on the bed. The Judys are talking quietly again. Mary is sitting. I reach into the pillowcase and pull out the notecards and the pen. I strangely miss the little girl. I'm looking forward to seeing her later.

Under Vic – Brother, I add two more lines:

Don't take pills
Trying to remember

I look at the notecard again. Now, when I see it, I'll remember that I'm not supposed to take my pills.

A thought occurs to me.

How am I going to remember to check the notecard?

I let out a frustrated sigh.

My eyes open. I hadn't realized I fell asleep. There's a pen on the bed, and a notecard on the floor. I reach down and pick up the card to read it.

The memory hits me like a bolt of lightning, and I put them both away as hastily as I can. I read the card one more time before shoving it back in my pillowcase.

When I look up, Mary is looking at me.

I turn my head. The Judys are asleep, their arms intertwined.

"What are you doing?" The voice sounds so odd coming from Mary.

I didn't know she spoke.

Wait, I must know that. How else would I know how she got here?

It's extremely uncanny to read notes I know I wrote, but I don't remember writing.

It's like reading letters from a time traveler.

"Trying to remember," I answer her.

She gives me a sad smile. "Don't give up," she whispers, then turns her attention back to staring at the wall.

A short time later, a nurse steps in. "Okay, ladies, activity time!"

The Judys wake up, and I go over to shake Mary and let her know that it's time to go.

Seven

Shuffling down the hallway, I can feel the memory of my task trying to escape again. I keep trying to rein it back in, but it slips away before I can find a way to hold on.

I sit down at a table that has a puzzle started, but I don't care about cars. I don't want to put the rest of this one together. I break the pieces back up and stick them in the box.

The actual picture is weird. I'm glad I'm putting it back.

Shuffling over to the shelf, I choose something happier. A picture of a playground, children swinging, laughing, and just generally in motion. It's a much happier scene than my current view of the back of everyone's matted, greasy heads.

I look down again. It makes me smile.

I sit back at the table and take the pieces out of the box. I sort them by color, by edge pieces, by pattern. It's hard work when you live in a cloud of fog.

Several times, I find myself staring at a piece instead of sorting it. Especially the children's faces. They look so happy.

When the nurse tells us that activity time is over, I have five puzzle pieces together. Maybe not the most efficient job, but I'm proud of how organized everything is. I'll pick it back up after dinner.

Dinner tonight is more mystery meat, but at least dessert is a Jell-O cup. Green is my favorite flavor. I'm scraping the bottom of my cup when I realize I'm being stared at. Looking up, I see Mary watching me. The Judys and Betty are chatting, and I'm missing the conversation.

That's strange. Mary doesn't usually do more than stare at the wall.

I put my spoon down on my tray, and it makes a plastic clanking noise. "What?" I ask Mary.

"You're trying not to forget." She frowns at me.

I get a chill. "What?" I say again. I'm confused, but also curious.

"You said you were trying to remember, but you're forgetting again. I can see it." Her face is flat. Serious.

"I… I'm sorry. I don't know what you're talking about." What does she think I'm forgetting? Am I forgetting?

I think hard. There's a flicker, but it's buried deep in my head, and it doesn't surface. I'm not sure what she means.

Mary shakes her head sadly at me. She doesn't say anything else and goes back to staring.

Judy 2 glances away from her conversation and asks, "What's wrong with you?" She's smoking a cigarette and flicks the ash into her Jell-O cup.

I don't know why you'd waste perfectly good Jell-O. "Nothing, I'm fine." I pick up my spoon and scrape the last dregs of flavor out of my cup.

"Okay, weirdo," Judy 2 laughs. She glances over at Mary, then turns back to her conversation with the others.

Alone with my thoughts, I wonder how Mary knows I'm forgetting something. I look around, trying to see through the haze of my meds. Everything looks normal. People shuffling around, outlines blurry. I look at my clothes. Slippers, robe, pants. All normal. Or at least, normal for this place.

What am I forgetting? What else have I done today? Before this, we had activity time.

What did I do?

I read magazines.

No.

I did a puzzle. Well, tried to.

I'm pleased with myself. I remember what I did before dinner.

Back in the activity room, I sit down at my puzzle. Everything is sorted just so. I look at the different piles. I'm happy with how precisely each one is organized. I pick up a piece that looks like it would fit with what is already put together. As I'm looking to see where it may fit, Nurse Delaney comes by to check on me.

"Hi, Nadia, how are you feeling tonight?" She smiles at me and puts her hand on my shoulder. "Great job on this puzzle so far! What a happy scene you picked."

"Thank you," I say. I feel like a child who received praise from their teacher. "I'm doing my best."

"You're doing really well, Nadia. Keep up the good work." She smiles again and then moves on to check on other patients.

I happily go back to my puzzle instead of watching *Mary Tyler Moore*. I try to put more pieces together, but a lot of them just don't fit quite right.

I realize I'm starting to get frustrated. Then I see her.

She's sitting in a chair with the patients, watching TV. She turns and looks at me, her braid swinging across her back. She smiles and waves at me, then turns back to the TV.

I sigh. I really should tell Dr. Herbert that I see her when my meds are wearing off, and that I'm seeing her a lot these days. But I really don't want him to up my meds. And I don't want her to go away either. I watch her, the light from the TV playing across her innocent face.

She looks over again, and I motion for her to come sit by me.

The little girl hops down off the chair and skips over to my table, taking a seat at my left side.

"Hi!" she says happily.

"Hi," I whisper as quietly as I can. "What are you doing here?"

She flashes a big smile at me. "I'm here to remind you, silly. You know that."

"I'm forgetting again, right?"

Her green eyes almost glow with happiness. "Yes! But you remembered that you're forgetting. And that's something!" She happily bounces in her chair.

"What am I forgetting?" I whisper again.

An orderly taps me on the shoulder. "Who are you talking to?"

My addled brain tries to think quickly. I pick up a puzzle piece to give myself a moment.

"Well?" he says. "Do I need to get a nurse?"

"No, no, I'm fine. I'm sorry if I was being too loud. I was frustrated that I couldn't find these pieces. I was talking to myself." I look up at him and give him my signature lopsided smile.

He nods. "Okay, just keep it down." Then he moves on.

I let out a breath. "You almost got me in trouble," I tell the little girl.

She looks solemn for a moment. "I'm sorry. I'm not trying to hurt you. I'm trying to help." Then she brightens again and continues bouncing in her chair. "I'm so glad you remembered that you're forgetting!"

"What am I forgetting?" I whisper again.

She stops bouncing. "I can't tell you. You have to figure it out on your own. You have to remember." She looks around for a clock. "I wonder what time it is?" Then she moves to a table with magazines. "Come sit here!"

I get up and shuffle over to the magazine table. I pick one up and pretend to read it. "Why are we here?" I whisper. It's easier to hide that I'm talking with a magazine in front of my face. I realize I'm not irritated like I typically am when the little girl is here.

"To help you remember, of course." She smiles at me. "Keep reading, you'll find it."

"Find what?"

Oops, forgot to whisper. I look up, but nobody heard me. The magazine must have muffled my voice a little.

I'm about to ask again what I'm looking for when I see it. A card, one that you fill out to subscribe to the publication. I have an odd feeling, like a thought is trying to push to the surface of my brain. It almost feels like physical pressure.

I look over at the little girl, but she's just sitting there, smiling at me. I take the card out of the magazine and hold it in my hand for a moment. What about this feels so familiar?

Nurse Delaney spots me and walks by. "You subscribing, Moren?" She laughs.

I laugh too at the absurdity of the question. "Probably not, Nurse Delaney. I would need money for that." Then it surfaces. The pen. I remember the pen. I look at the little girl, shocked.

She smiles at me and nods. "I knew you could do it."

Nurse Delaney's smile falters. "Are you okay, hon?" she starts to step toward me.

I smile at her. "I'm fine. Just thinking about which magazine I want." I laugh again, but it's hollow. I just want her to go away so I can think.

She chuckles and walks away to check on another patient.

I hold the card in my hand. I can't believe I did it. I don't remember what the card in my pillowcase says, but I know that it's there. I'm going to check when we go back to our rooms. I need to do it before evening meds, or I'll forget again.

I look around, then put the card in my waistband. I don't want to forget. I take another card and hold it in my hands, behind a magazine, until TV time is over.

Eight

Out in the hall on the walk back to 108, I struggle to hold the thought in. I don't want to let it go.

The card at my waistband shifts and pokes me. It's a reminder that I can't let myself forget. I'm the first one back to the room, and I rip the other card out of my pillowcase.

Reading it, I smile. I remember. I leave the blank one in my waistband.

The Judys filter in, and Mary is right behind them. They all sit on their beds, waiting for meds.

A nurse I don't recognize flies into the room, handing out paper cups. She does a cursory check of my mouth and then flies back out. They must be short-staffed today.

I reach up and pull the pill out of the space between my upper lip and gums. Tossing it into my pillowcase with the last one, I look at the little girl triumphantly.

She looks happy, too. Stretching out on the end of my cot, she relaxes, hands behind her head.

I look up, and Mary is staring at me. After a nod and a small smile, she goes back to looking straight ahead.

A short while later, it's time for bed, but I don't want to sleep. I know if I do, I'll forget again. I need to figure out a way to remember when I wake up, at least for tomorrow. I have a suspicion that if I can get the meds out of my system, I won't have such a hard time remembering anymore.

With drowsiness taking over and a lack of a better idea, I decide to leave the blank card in my waistband.

Hopefully, I'll notice it first thing, and it will jog my memory.

I wake, and it's still dark outside.

What was that noise?

I'm disoriented. It's dark, and my meds are wearing off. Looking at the foot of the bed, I can see the little girl sitting up, bathed in moonlight.

I glance at the Judys, but they're both sleeping soundly. Looking toward the door, I see that Mary is awake and trying to see out the small window.

She turns and sees me. "Did you hear it?" she asks.

"I heard something," I say.

She turns back to the door. "It was the screams. They're doing it again." She tries once more to look out the little window, but it's evident she won't be able to see anything. She gives up and goes back to sit on her bed.

"What are they doing?" I ask. I feel clearer than I have in a while, and the combination of my brain trying to jump-start itself and the sounds of the screams makes me afraid of what she's going to say.

I feel raw, on edge.

Mary looks at me, then looks away. "I don't know exactly what they're doing, but I know it's wrong. It's something they can't do in the daylight." She looks back at me, face guarded. Is she testing the waters to see if I believe her?

I'm terrified, but I want to know more. I want to know what she knows. "I think you're right. How can we find out?" I go over to the door and test the handle. It's locked, as usual. When I turn around, she's looking at me.

"Do you really want to find out?" She's tense, like I just asked an unwarranted personal question.

I look out into the hall. It's very dark, and I can't see anything either. "I don't know," I tell her honestly. "But doesn't it feel wrong?" I turn back to face her. "How can they do this to people?"

She shakes her head. "I don't know," she replies softly.

I go back to sit on my bed. The little girl is looking at me, wide-eyed. She doesn't look scared, but she isn't the happy, bouncy version of herself that she normally is. I can't talk to her in front of Mary, it will just confirm how crazy I am.

The three of us sit, listening to the screams, until they subside. A short time later, we hear the squeak of the gurney and soft moaning as it passes our room.

I wake in the morning with a slight headache. Something is different. The sun feels too bright, and the orderly yelling, "Wake up! Med rounds!" is too loud.

I roll onto my side, and a piece of cardstock pokes me. I lift my shirt, and it's sticking out of my waistband.

That's right! My note to myself. I don't remember what it says, but I know it's there. Doing my best impression of hurrying, I find the card in my pillowcase and manage to read it before the nurse comes in.

Shoving the card back into my pillowcase, I sit at the foot of the bed and wait for my turn. Looking around, Mary sits and stares at nothing. Judy 2 is taking her meds, and Judy 1 is waiting quietly for her turn.

I try not to fidget while waiting. I wonder briefly how many doses I've skipped. The card doesn't say, just that I should avoid the meds. I should start counting. When the nurse leaves, I'll add a tick mark and make a note to keep count.

The nurse approaches and hands me my paper cup. I'm nervous, and drop it. The pill skitters across the floor, and the nurse looks at me like I did it on purpose. She picks up the pill from the floor, shoves it back into the cup, and hands it to me.

I obediently put it into my mouth, then show her it's empty.

She moves on, but her irritation provoked by my carelessness is evident in her movements.

When she leaves the room, I reach up and take the pill out of my mouth. The little girl smiles and jumps up and down. "Yay! You did it!"

"I did," I say to her quietly. I glance around. The Judys are involved in their own conversation, and Mary doesn't look up. "Do you know how many times I've skipped?" I ask her.

She shakes her head. "I only know what you know. I know it's not a lot, based on how you feel right now." She smiles. "But you're getting better. You'll start remembering."

I smile too, even though I feel strange. "Why do I feel so… odd? Almost… bad?" I whisper to her.

"The meds have to leave your system," she says. "It may take a little while. You've been on them a long time now."

That makes sense, but it also creates some problems.

I feel shaky, the light hurts, and sounds are amplified. I'm going to have to be especially careful not to seem agitated, even if I am. I know how quickly they'll medicate me if I seem too aware.

An orderly opens the door and yells, "Breakfast!" Then leaves it open behind him. I get up and start to walk toward the door, then realize how difficult this task is going to be. I begin to shuffle slowly toward the dining hall. I'm going to have to put on the act of my life, while also fighting detox from my meds.

I shuffle down the hall and start to notice all the small details that were previously outside of my limited, foggy view of my world. Passing the nurses' station on this floor, I see a clock on the wall. A typewriter. A counter with a phone with multiple lines. They even have a coffee pot. It makes sense, especially for the night shift.

I shudder. Thinking of the night shift reminds me of the screams.

I see a nurse looking at me. I drop my eyes and stare at the slippers of the woman in front of me, trying to look foggy. I have to be careful not to look too alert or curious.

She doesn't stop me, so I think I'm in the clear.

I shuffle into the dining hall and get in line, grabbing a tray. I do my best to avoid eye contact with anyone, including the servers. It smells much worse in here than usual, and my stomach turns.

Spotting the Judys and Betty at a nearby table, I slide in next to Betty. "Mary's not here?" I ask.

"Who cares?" Judy 2 replies, laughing.

Judy 1 slaps her on the arm lightly. "Be nice!"

She rolls her eyes and goes back to eating her breakfast.

I eat quietly, listening.

The Judys and Betty are talking about hairstyles. The ones they used to have and the ones they've seen in magazines in the activity room that they'd love to try.

I briefly wonder how long they've been here. How long *I've* been here.

This food is awful, but I'm starving, and I polish off my tray. Thinking about it after, it probably wasn't a great idea since I've only ever picked at meals as long as I can remember. It's going to be an adjustment to settle into my new acting role. I'm lucky that the nurse only stopped by once at the beginning to see how everyone was doing.

Shuffling back to my room, I'm trying to spy without looking like I'm spying. When I pass the procedure room, the door is open. I try to notice what I can without looking suspicious. There isn't much to see at a glance. A gurney with leather restraints attached. A movable floor lamp. A tray that likely holds tools while the room is occupied. The same overhead fluorescent lights, though they're off right now. The room gives me the creeps.

My stomach has settled, but the lights still feel too bright, and every sound is exaggerated. It's going to take some real patience to get through this part, but I know I need to. I want to know who I am and where I came from.

I realize that I remember things. A lot of things that I normally wouldn't. I remember waking up this morning. I remember the notecard and even some of what's written on it, though not everything. I remember walking by the nurses' station this morning and noticing things I hadn't before. Most importantly, I remember that I'm not going to take my pill.

I smile slightly, glad to be remembering again.

Shuffling into my room, I sit at the edge of the bed and wait for Dr. Herbert and his nurse to arrive. I glance at Mary. She's lying down in bed, sleeping. Maybe she's sick today, which would explain why she wasn't at breakfast.

The Judys come in and sit on their beds.

The little girl smiles at me from the floor. She doesn't need to speak; we're on the same page now.

As I'm thinking about how I need to make a note of the doses I know I've skipped, Dr. Herbert and a nurse come in and start with the Judys.

I observe the nurse. Blonde, thirties, tall. I watch her in my peripheral vision. She seems to have an attitude, like she's better than this. She listens and makes notes as Dr.

Herbert talks, and then hands out paper cups, but she looks like she'd rather be anywhere else.

When the pair walks over to me, I slowly glance up at her name tag. *Rourke.* This is good information. I need to remember to write this down when they leave.

Dr. Herbert rattles off his usual interlude. *Nadia Moren. Female. thirty-four years old.*

I listen patiently and try to look dazed.

He doesn't engage with me, and the nurse hands me my paper cup. She doesn't wait to make sure I take the pill. She follows him right out the door, leaving the paper cup with me.

I'm shocked, but glad. Now I have somewhere to store my unused pills. I didn't even have to get the nasty taste in my mouth today.

Taking the cards out of my pillowcase, I read through them, then add to the list:

Nurses – Rourke
Skipped Pills – III

I look at my drawing of the little girl. It's good. I wonder where I learned to draw like that. Is it a hobby?

I glance over at the Judys, cuddling together, sharing a pillow and blanket. Mary is still asleep.

Taking the three pills I've collected out of my pillowcase, I slip them into the little cup, then get down on the floor. I squeeze the sides of the cup together so the pills don't fall out and slide it under one of the mattress springs. I sit on the bed and bounce slightly, then check to make sure they didn't fall.

They didn't; they're secure.

My stomach is slightly upset again, whether from the bad food or the detox, I can't tell. I decide that a nap sounds like a great idea, especially after being up half the night. Lying on my bed, I drift off to sleep.

It's nice knowing that when I wake up, I'll remember.

Nine

It's a beautiful day. Late spring. The midday sun shines brightly on the wet pebbles that line the shore. I'm sitting in an Adirondack chair, a blanket loosely wrapped around my body. I don't really need it for warmth, but it's comforting all the same.

I hear a noise over the waves and look up, smiling. It's Vic.

Or at least, I think it's Vic. His face is blurry, but I know it's him. His eyebrows give it away.

"Don't get up," he says, bending down to embrace me. When we part, he sits in the chair beside me. "You're doing it." He smiles at me. "You're breaking through."

I look at him, puzzled. "Breaking through what?"

"The fog," he says simply, looking out over the water.

I look at him like he's crazy. "What fog? It's a beautiful day."

He turns back to me, eyebrows practically touching. "Do you hear it?"

"Hear what?" I can feel goosebumps rising on my arms, the hair at the back of my neck standing up. I can sense that there is danger somewhere near.

He takes my hand gently. It's warm and dry, comforting. "The screams. Can you hear them?"

Suddenly, I do hear them, far in the distance. Screams of terror and pain. I look back at Vic, shocked.

He nods. "You need to remember."

Now I'm angry. "I'm trying to remember!" Standing up, I throw my blanket off.

I realize I'm not holding Vic's hand. I'm in a straitjacket.

I look out at the water. The sea is angry. Dark clouds furiously frame it.

The boom of thunder can be heard, rolling in as the screams grow louder.

Lightning strikes, and I wake up.

Ten

I sit up, sweating.

The dream was so vivid. I don't even remember the last time I had a dream. This one was strange. Somehow freeing, but claustrophobic at the same time.

I look at the wall, then curse this place for not having clocks. I can't have been asleep for long. They should be by soon to bring us to OT.

Mary is still asleep in her bed. She doesn't sit up when an orderly flings open the door. "OT! Let's go! OT time!"

The Judys and I file out of the room, following the crowd. I look back once at Mary as I'm leaving. I hope she's okay.

We shuffle down the corridor, past the nurses' station. Nobody is there, so I stop a moment to take a look around. I stand there pretending to be dazed, but looking for whatever else I can see that escaped me last time. On the far side of the desk, there's a keyring hanging from a peg on the wall with many keys on it.

My eyes go wide as I realize it's a master keyring. It holds the keys to all the doors on this floor. I shuffle off, trying to process what I just learned.

The patients are herded into a room I don't recognize. There are long tables set up. Every few feet, there is a basket with thread, scraps of fabric, and sewing needles.

We all choose a seat, and I notice that Nurse Delaney and Nurse Rourke are both here.

Delaney can't go on my list; she notices everything.

We're instructed to thread the needle and then practice stitching the fabric scraps together. I sit as still as possible, trying to look dazed, while I gauge how everyone else is doing with this task. I don't want to outpace my peers too much and be noticed.

Picking up a needle, I try to thread it. My hands are shaking. "Shit," I mumble to myself.

I try again, but I'm too shaky to get the thread through the needle. I look up. Both nurses' backs are to me. I steal my neighbor's threaded needle and replace it with my empty one.

She turns to me slowly, sloth-like. She's angry. "Heeey!" she says loudly.

I put on my foggiest face and turn toward her, just as the nurses are looking to see what's going on. "What?" I ask groggily.

"You stole my needle!" she says, upset, as she points to the thread in my hands.

"What?" I say again.

Nurse Delaney comes over to diffuse the situation. "Okay, ladies, let's not argue. Theresa, you're holding your needle. You just need to thread it." She points to the needle in Theresa's hand.

"Oh, right," Theresa says slowly. "Thanks." She turns back to her fabric scraps.

I spend the next two hours trying to look like a drugged-up woman sewing. I pace myself, constantly checking the work of the patients around me. I try to land somewhere in the middle of the pack. Not too little done, and not too much. When we're told it's time to put needles down, I've sewn a very rough two patches into one patch. I realize how mentally exhausting it's going to be playing at being medicated.

The group shuffles off to the dining hall. I go through the line to get my lunch tray. I see Mary and the Judys sitting together. Mary isn't mentally present, but I'm glad she's back. Betty spots us and sits down. The gang is back together again.

I try to eat more slowly than I did at breakfast. I need to leave at least half of everything on my plate to be believable.

Betty is talking about how she's expecting a visit from her husband this week. She's hoping he'll bring her kid with him. Maybe she can convince him she's okay now, so that she can come home.

I feel bad for her. I can't imagine being in that position. I don't think Betty is crazy. A lot of women have a hard time adjusting to motherhood. I think society just doesn't understand why quite yet.

As I'm shuffling down the hall toward my room for quiet hours, I'm hit with the smell of disinfectant. I notice the doors to the procedure room are wide open, and two orderlies are cleaning everything. They're probably getting it ready for a patient. A chill goes through me that I can't control. I shuffle a little quicker to get past the room. I don't like to look in there.

Stepping into 108, I'm met with a confusing sight. Mary is on her bed as usual, but there is a nurse and two orderlies in the room. Judy 2 is yelling, and Judy 1 is crying as the orderlies drag her out.

"Nothing happened! She was crying, and I was comforting her!" Judy 2 is screaming at the nurse. "You got this all wrong! Stop! Where are you taking her?!" She has tears forming in her eyes, but her anger won't let them fall.

Judy 1 sobs quietly as the orderlies drag her out into the hallway. "Come on, you disgusting dyke. The doctor will fix you up alright," says one of them.

The other chimes in, "It's a shame, you're a pretty one too."

And just like that, Judy 1 is gone.

Judy 2 loses it and lunges at the nurse. Two more orderlies run in from the hallway and hold her down while the nurse administers a sedative right into her thigh. Within fifteen seconds, Judy 2 is lying on the bed, immobile.

I'm standing just inside the door, unsure what to do. My mind is nearly free of the effects of the meds, but I hadn't prepared for a situation like this, and I don't know how to handle it. The nurse looks over at me, then instructs me to lie down in my bed.

I shuffle over to the bed and sit. I must be feeling brave, because I ask, "What… what happened?"

She's already halfway out the door, but she turns back and looks at me for a moment, then decides to answer my question. "I caught them in here kissing." Her face twists in disgust. "If you see anything like that happen, you make sure to tell the nurses, okay?" She disappears without waiting for an answer.

When I'm sure she's gone, I go over to check on Judy 2. She's near catatonic, but tears spill over her cheeks. I wipe them away, but they keep coming. She's lying half off the bed, so I pull her into the center and try to make her comfortable.

"I'm sorry," I whisper to her, pushing her hair back from her forehead. I'm not sure what else to say. I can't tell her it will be alright.

We would both know it's a lie.

Eleven

After quiet hours, I shuffle off to the activity room.

I don't really want to leave Judy 2, but I don't have a choice.

When I open the door to leave, Mary follows me.

I sigh heavily. Even though I think Mary may not respond, I ask her, "Did you see all of that happen?"

She replies quietly, "Only some of it. I was lost in my own thoughts and only saw after the orderlies came in."

"I feel like I need to do something for the Judys. I don't know what, but I feel so powerless." I can feel myself getting agitated. I know I need to calm down, or I'll be outed, forced to take meds I don't want.

"I don't think there is anything you can do for them. The damage is done now," Mary says.

She's right. I may be more lucid than I was, but I'm still just a loon in an asylum. I can't change anyone's fate.

When we walk into the activity room, we separate. Mary goes to sit in front of the TV, and I look around, wondering how I'm going to spend the next two hours without it driving me crazier. I notice that one of the magazine tables has been cleared. The old magazines have been replaced by crayons, markers, and colored pencils. There are blank sheets to scribble on and coloring pages to fill in.

I make my way over there at my fastest fake shuffle. There are four seats at the table, and I narrowly beat out another woman for the last one. I sit and pretend I didn't see her. She looks disappointed, but shuffles away to go watch TV instead.

Two of the women at the table are holding crayons or markers and just staring at a coloring page. Another is actively coloring, but is turning the sky in the picture pink. Maybe she likes sunsets.

I take a blank piece of paper and hold it in my hands for a moment. Is it weird that I kind of want to smell it? I decide against it.

I pick up a colored pencil and start to sketch a face. Even with my shakiness, I begin seeing Judy 1 appear on the page. That might not be the best idea right now. I change up some of her features to make it look more like a generic woman that I don't know.

One of the nurses walking by gives the table a cursory glance. She stops abruptly and picks up my drawing, looking surprised. "This is really good, Moren! Did you use to be an artist?" She stares at the picture, trying to decide whether she recognizes the face.

"I don't remember," I tell her honestly. "I don't know what I did before I came here."

"Well, whatever it was, you've definitely drawn before," she says, putting the picture down. She briefly looks over the childish coloring of the other three ladies, but doesn't check on them or pay too much attention.

I glance at her name tag. *Trevany*. I'll have to add her to my list.

I grab another sheet of paper as a thought hits me. I should try to smuggle a real piece of paper, also maybe a pencil or crayon, back to the room. It would be easier to have a single list than multiple magazine cards. And I could have a backup if my pen breaks.

I sketch as I consider how I can pull that off without being seen. I can feel the wheels turning in my head clearly now. The fog is nearly gone, and once the tremors and headache subside, I should be nearly normal again. Well, normal for me, anyway. I do wonder what will happen once the meds are fully out of my system.

What did Dr. Herbert say during rounds this morning? Something about psychosis and agitation. I look up, and the little girl is sitting on the floor nearby. She appears to be reading a comic book, but she sees me looking and smiles.

Well, there's the psychosis part of my diagnosis. Have I always seen her?

I have been a little bit agitated, but I want to blame that on trying to detox from my meds. I'm hoping it gets a little better once I'm past it. What am I going to be like once I'm back to my own normal?

That's the question of the day, I guess.

I look down. I had been letting my mind wander while I was sketching. The face looking back at me seems familiar, but I can't place it. It's someone from my past, but I don't know who.

I stare at the picture, trying to will the memory forward. My brain has been drug-addled for so long that it doesn't surface.

My fists clench. I can feel myself starting to get upset. I know I need to stay calm.

I look at the little girl. Her eyes are wide. She can see me, feel me slipping.

"Don't do it," she says. She's calm.

I'm not.

I put my head in my hands, trying to suppress the fury that I feel. It's rising inside me. My best efforts can't contain it. I push away from the table, seeing red.

"Why can't I remember!" I yell with my eyes shut and my heart beating faster. I'm full of barely concealed rage. I open my eyes and tear the picture in two.

Looking up, Nurse Delaney and two orderlies are headed for me. I stand up and scream "NO!" at them as I attempt to get away. The orderlies pin me, and I can see Nurse Delaney arranging the needle. They're not even planning to take me to the hallway this time.

I feel the icy hotness of the drug enter my leg. It spread outward to my feet, my hands, and my face. I'm beginning to pass out when I see the little girl's face hovering above me.

She's saying something.

What is it?

As I slip into semi-consciousness, I hear her.

"I won't let you forget this time."

Twelve

I come to groggily.

Where am I?

Slowly lifting my head, I realize I'm in 108. My arms are heavy, and my head feels like it's full of cotton.

Turning slightly toward the window, I see the sky outside has darkened, but not gone completely black.

Why am I in bed at this time of day? I try to think.

What do I remember?

It hits me like a bolt of lightning.

Oh my God, Judy 1.

I sit up as quickly as I can, and the room spins for a moment. I look around, but nobody is here.

I think harder. I can't remember anything after Judy 1 was taken away. Did I react poorly, and they dosed me?

Judging from the sky, it's either dinner time or nearing the end of it.

"I'm not going to let you forget this time. You know that." She's sitting on Judy 1's bed, next to me.

The fog in my head is still there, but now I have a slight memory of her telling me this. "What am I forgetting?" The world around me is blurry, but the little girl isn't.

She tilts her head and smiles. "You know. You can remember. I know you can."

I close my eyes. What is the last thing I remember? Judy 1, right. What happened next? I feel the straining sensation in my head, but it surfaces.

Judy 2 was dosed. That's right. I smile, not because of Judy, but because I remembered.

I look at the little girl. She gestures for me to continue.

Closing my eyes again, I strain to think for a moment, and the next memory surfaces. I went to the activity room. There were colored pencils.

I open them, and the little girl is smiling ear to ear.

"I knew you could do it! What else?"

The rest comes in a single flash, like a dam let loose, and the floodwaters have washed over my brain.

The drawing. The paper. The face. The nurse dosing me. I remember I'm not taking my pills, that I'm keeping a list, that I'm a watcher now. I'm noticing things.

The little girl gets up and does a cartwheel. I notice she's not in her green dress. She's wearing playclothes. A t-shirt with a peace sign and leggings.

My head is foggy, but I remember now. They tried to make me forget, but I won't let them anymore.

A short time later, Judy 2 enters the room, red-eyed and disoriented.

Mary is right behind her. They sit on their respective beds. Mary is quiet, as usual. She gives me a small head tilt and a sad smile before beginning her descent into her own head for the evening.

Judy 2 lies down and puts her face into her pillow. I can hear her crying quietly.

The little girl goes over and sits on the end of Judy 2's bed. It's a sweet gesture of moral support that my brain has created. I know that the nurse will be in soon with rounds, and I can't physically comfort her like I wish I could.

A nurse scurries in. Nurse Trevany.

I remember her.

She asks Judy 2 to sit, and when she doesn't answer, she skips her and comes to me. She hurriedly hands me my cup, then takes just a cursory glance in my mouth. I'm pretty sure the pill could still have been in there, and she wouldn't have noticed.

When she's done, she skips Mary completely and goes back to Judy 2. She is still not budging. Nurse Trevany leaves the room and comes back with a needle, giving Judy 2 a dose that way. She then leaves without giving Mary her rounds.

I look over to Mary, who is aware of what just happened. She looks back and shrugs. I think we both know she didn't really want the meds anyway.

I take out my list and add Nurse Trevany to it. As I'm writing, I notice my hands aren't shaking anymore. That's probably not a good sign; it means I need to start my detox over.

The evening wears on, and a while later, it's time for lights out.

Nurse Trevany pokes her head in and turns off the light, shutting the door behind her.

My heart beats faster. Did she not lock it? I didn't hear the normal "click" sound that it usually makes.

I lie in bed, thinking.

Could I realistically do what I'm thinking of doing?

The little girl is at my side. "You could. You'd have to be careful."

She's right. I could. But am I brave enough? Do I want to know what causes the screams that badly? I shudder, thinking about what could happen if I'm caught.

I lie in the dark, waiting. I know my sense of time is blurred because of the dose I had earlier. This excursion is going to be more difficult because I'm not fully out of the fog again yet. I stay in the same spot, awake, for what must be hours.

Finally, I hear them. The screams. Floating down the hall like the ghosts of our collectively forgotten aspirations.

I get out of bed and go to the window. The hall is dark, just like it always is. I look back. Judy 2 and Mary are sound asleep. They didn't hear them.

Putting my hand on the doorknob, part of me hopes it won't turn.

It does anyway.

I'm in the hall. My palms are sweaty, despite it being cool out here. I take a step in the direction of the procedure room, then another.

I have to remember now *not* to shuffle. I don't want my footsteps to be heard, echoing down the empty hallway.

I walk as quietly as possible until I come to the nurses' station. It's thankfully empty.

Looking around, I notice more things I hadn't seen in my cursory investigation before.

Off to the left of the station is a doorway. The small room has a door, but it's left open. The sign above says "Records Room." This must be where they keep the ever-growing patient charts and histories for each person.

I walk over quietly and take a peek inside. The room is very small and lined floor to ceiling with filing cabinets. There's a moving ladder to access the drawers in the upper cabinets. Most of them are labeled as expected. "Patients A-C," "Patients T-Z." But some have less straightforward labeling. "Research Studies" and "Patient Outcomes" are two that catch my eye.

I don't want to loiter here too long in case the night nurse is on her way back. I step out into the hallway and continue my journey.

I want to know what is causing the screams.

I start to shuffle down the hall and stop, realizing again that I have to be quiet.

There's still nobody around. It seems strange. I know everyone should be asleep, but it's a hospital. Don't patients have episodes at all hours?

Suddenly, I hear what sounds like a drill starting up. A moment later, screaming fills the hallway.

It's eerie, the hallway filled with sounds of machinery and pain.

The procedure room is about twenty feet away, on my right. I look around, and there is still not a person to be found. They must all be in that room.

Tiptoeing as quietly as I can, I inch up to the double doors and peek through the window, trying to avoid being seen.

It's bright in there, and my eyes have to adjust to the blinding light. The screaming has subsided for now, but I can hear moaning, the staff talking quietly, and metal hand tools clinking as they're passed around.

My eyes focus first on the gurney. The patient is strapped down, arms and legs held in leather straps crudely attached to the bed. I can't see their face, but they don't move much. They must be at least partially drugged. A doctor with a nurse by his side is at the patient's head, working from a small, square area that has been shaved. From this angle, I can't tell what they're doing, and I'm grateful that I can't see.

I don't need specifics. I've seen enough. The smell of burnt flesh, metal, and isopropyl alcohol waft from the room. I need to get out of here before I'm sick.

I rush back down the hall as silently as I can. Quietly opening the door to 108, I close it carefully behind me.

I sink to the floor with my back against it, heart hammering in my chest.

Was all of that real?

I'm crazy. Maybe I made it up? Or at least some of it?

My breath comes in fast bursts.

My heart is racing.

I'm lightheaded.

"Slow down," I say out loud. Whether I'm talking to my lungs or my heart, I'm not sure.

The room spins.

I lay down on the floor, waiting for this awful feeling to pass.

Thirteen

Opening my eyes, daylight is pouring through the dirty window. My heart rate and breathing seem to have normalized.

As I stand up to go sit on my bed, the door opens.

I surprise an orderly who wasn't expecting to see someone standing near the door before wake up.

"Wake up!" he yells anyway, "Morning meds!" before slamming the door behind him.

Walking over to my bed, I glance at Judy 2. She doesn't appear to have moved since yesterday. She's still lying face down on her pillow. Looking towards Mary's bed, she's sitting up and lets out a large yawn. Neither of them appears to know about my escapades from last night.

I feel clearer again; the dose that they gave me during activity time yesterday has worn off. I'm shaky, and my head hurts, but my mind is sharp again. It's good to know that the longer I go without meds, the easier it is to recover from a single dose.

Now I have to work on recovering my memories from before Ravensbrook. The wheels in my head start turning as I wonder how I'm going to accomplish that.

A nurse hurries in with everyone's meds. She starts with me today. I never noticed before that there isn't a consistent pattern of who goes first. She hands me my cup, then turns to make a note on the chart. She turns back and takes the paper cup away. She didn't even check my mouth.

I glance at her name tag. Nurse White. I'll note that after she leaves.

She moves on to Judy next.

I'm holding the pill in my hand. I didn't even need to pretend to swallow it. She didn't seem concerned about whether I even took it.

Once she leaves, I drop to the floor and add it to my collection under the mattress. There are six pills now. Six times I've fought back and won. It feels like a victory, even if it's a small one. I dig in my pillowcase for the note card and pen, adding Nurse White's name. I also shiver as I add:

Screams – Procedure room – Surgeries

I don't fully understand yet what I saw, but I know it was enough to turn my stomach. And it seems that Mary is right; whatever they're doing, it's something they can't do in the light of day.

I shuffle down the hallway toward breakfast. As I pass the nurses' station, I take a look at the door to the records room. It's closed now.

A chill runs down my spine, though I don't exactly know why.

My shuffling continues, and I spot the procedure room up ahead. The hall smells of strong disinfectant this morning. The metal and flesh scent, gone for now.

My stomach heaves slightly as I think again about what I witnessed.

Breakfast is quiet. Judy 1 is missing, Judy 2 stares at her tray but doesn't eat. Mary looks ahead, but occasionally breaks her blank stare to look at Judy 2 with concern. Betty tries to make small talk, but with nobody else willing to chat, she decides to eat quietly.

I arrive back at 108 just ahead of Mary, with Judy 2 trailing behind. We sit on our beds, waiting for morning rounds. The door opens, but instead of Doctor Herbert, it's a nurse and two orderlies. They escort Judy 1 back into the room.

She looks different. Pale. Her face is drawn, and there's a shaved patch on the side of her blonde head. A small wound that's been stitched up.

Judy 2 sits up suddenly, alert.

The nurse tells Judy 1 to sit down, and she does, obediently. The orderlies are dismissed. The nurse stays by the bed.

"How are you feeling, Judith?" the nurse asks. Her face softens, as if she's talking to a small child.

"I'm fine, thank you." Judy 1's voice is flat, emotionless, and small. She stares straight ahead at the buttons on the nurse's uniform.

I feel a pang of fear. Something about Judy 1 doesn't sit right.

"Okay. Judith, we're going to let you rest in your room today and continue recovering. We'll be checking on you periodically and will have your meals delivered here. You have a diaper for now, but once the sedation clears, you'll be able to use the restroom again. Do you understand?" She holds the clipboard on her hip, tilting her head to see if Judy 1 understands what she just told her.

"I understand." Judy 1 says, emotionless.

"Why don't you lie down, dear, and get more comfortable?" The nurse helps her onto the bed and lays her head on the pillow.

She complies without an argument, just lying there. Eyes open.

"I'll be back in a bit to check on you, Judith, okay?"

"Okay." Judy 1 replies. She doesn't blink or move. Just stares.

The nurse leaves, and before the door is even closed, Judy 2 jumps across the bed to hug her. "What happened? My God, Judy, what did they do to you!?"

Judy 1 makes eye contact with her and gives her a small smile that doesn't reach her eyes. "I'm fine. Thanks for asking."

"FINE? You're FINE? You don't seem FINE, Judy! What the hell happened?" Judy 2 is beside herself, worked into a frenzy. Tears well in her eyes, and she punches her pillow as anger bubbles over.

Judy 1 looks at her, and a small frown appears on her face. "Judy, you shouldn't get so upset. Things are fine. I'm okay. The doctor gave me a small procedure to help with my urges, that's all." She smiles again politely.

"Are you fucking serious?!" Judy 2 is shouting now. "They scrambled your brain because of *me*?" She can't contain the tears any longer, and they roll down her face with reckless abandon. "I love you, Judy. I'm so fucking sorry I let this happen." She sits hard on her bed, head in her hands, sobbing. "I can't believe I let this happen. I'm sorry that I'm broken, and I took you down with me."

An orderly swings the door open. It's one of the men who took Judy 1 away yesterday. A malicious smile crosses his face as he takes in the scene and realizes what's happening.

"What's wrong, dyke? Mad that the doc fixed up your toy?" He sneers at Judy 2. "She's not broken anymore, now she's in perfect shape. If she ever gets out of here, she can get herself a man to take care of her." He crosses his arms, pleased at the damage his words are doing to Judy 2.

Judy 1 continues lying on the bed, facing Judy 2 but not looking at her. Her face is vacant, vapid. A shell of who she was only yesterday.

Judy 2 looks up from her hands, and the fury in her eyes is palpable. She lunges at him and knocks him to the floor.

The orderly is shocked by the attack. He tries to grab Judy 2's arms, but her anger is so great that she overpowers him and gets her hands around his neck.

Mary is sitting on her bed, shocked, but not moving.

I'm also motionless, unsure what to do.

Judy 1 lies in bed, staring at nothing.

Hearing the struggle, a nurse pokes her head in. Her eyes go wide. "ORDERLIES!" she screams, and three of them rush into the room.

It takes the strength of all three to pull Judy 2 off the man, and they only succeed after the nurse gives Judy 2 an injection. As her body starts to go limp, she releases the neck of the man, and he scrambles to his feet, wheezing.

He slaps her, hard, across the face as she's losing consciousness. Two of the orderlies take his arms and help him out into the hallway. Another comes in and helps the last to drag Judy 2 out of the room, with the nurse following behind.

The room is quiet again. It's just Judy 1, Mary, and me. Mary and I stare at each other, not knowing what to say. I look back at Judy 1, and she's still lying there.

"Judy?" I say quietly. "Are you really okay?" Everything in me knows she's not. Maybe she's physically fine, but mentally she's not the same woman she was.

She glances at me and smiles, though it doesn't meet her eyes. "Yes, thanks, Nadia. I'm okay."

Turning back to Mary, I finally find some words. "There has to be something we can do. We can't leave her like this." My own eyes have filled with tears. Of sadness, frustration, and terror.

Mary looks at me. "There isn't anything we can do. We both know that. There's no fixing what's broken now." She looks over at Judy 1, sadness in her eyes.

This place is more dangerous than I realized. I know I'm crazy, for sure. But I don't belong here.

None of us do.

Fourteen

Mary and I shuffle down the hall to OT. Today, the room has been turned into an art room. Not just the coloring table in the activity room, but paints, canvases, and large pieces of clay are everywhere.

My frayed nerves are glad to have a task to focus on.

Without one, I risk crying over the Judys, and being dosed again or thrown into seclusion for being emotional.

I try my hand at shaping clay. I'm not good at it, though what I make slightly resembles a vase if you tilt your head the right way.

Painting is next. I feel very artistic with my palette, my paintbrush spreading color over the white canvas. I can almost picture myself sipping coffee, wearing a beret in Paris, a cigarette hanging out of the side of my mouth. But alas, my painting also isn't great. It's better than the clay, but that's not saying much.

I sit down at a table to draw, and faces appear as if by magic. I know I don't remember my past, but I must have sketched a lot. The muscle memory kicking in is so strange. I don't even know how I'm doing it, just that I let it happen, and when I focus my eyes, there's a face.

I look down again. It's the same woman I drew the other day. I remind myself that it's okay to be unsure who she is. I take a deep breath to remain calm. I don't need to get agitated and dosed again. If I can stay lucid and drug-free, I have time to put the pieces together.

Rome wasn't built in a day, and I'm not going to reclaim my past in a single one either.

I set the page aside and continue drawing. More faces emerge. Two men I don't recognize, another woman, and then weirdly, Nurse Delaney. I look up. She's walking around the room, supervising. Stopping here and there to instill praise on patients who look like they may need a boost.

That's strange. She is the nurse that I see the most, maybe that's why? I'm still puzzling over this mystery when she walks up behind me.

"Oh, Wow! This looks just like me, Nadia!" She picks up the drawing, looking delighted. "You just drew this just now?"

I try to sound far away, foggy. "Oh… yeah, I guess so."

She's beaming down at me. "You have quite a talent!" She puts the picture down and then announces to the room. "OT time is over, everyone! Time to clean up for lunch!"

"Nurse Delaney?" I say, still trying to speak slowly, slurring some of the sounds together. "Can I keep these?"

She looks back at me. "Of course, hon, of course." She walks away to help rinse out palettes and clean clay-covered hands.

At lunch, I'm quiet again. It's just Betty, Mary, and me at the table

"Where are Judy and Judy?" Betty asks, concerned.

I put my fork down, and my eyes start to tear up. I have to use every ounce of energy I have not to cry at the table.

Betty's eyes go wide. "What? What happened?" She leans in, desperate to find out what she's missed.

I look over at Mary.

Betty does too, but Mary doesn't speak.

"Ugh," I start, unsure whether she even knew why Judy 1 was missing yesterday.

"Blonde Judy had a procedure to "fix" her because of brunette Judy. Not sure if you knew they were… more than friends. Blonde Judy is resting in our room; brunette Judy is probably in seclusion for attacking an orderly who provoked her." I feel bad delivering the news this matter-of-factly.

Betty's already wide eyes widen even further. "Are you serious?" she whisper-yells.

A nurse looks up, and Betty looks down at her plate, pushing her food around with the fork.

When enough time has passed, she looks back up. "Did they lobotomize her?" She also has tears in her eyes.

"I don't know what they did, but she isn't the same now. She's childlike and very quiet. Keeps saying she's 'fine' when we know she's anything but fine." I sigh and put my head in my hands. "It's terrifying that they could do that to her. I don't even think there is anything wrong with Judy." I pick my fork back up and push my food around as a nurse makes her way around our table.

"What about other Judy?" Betty asks. "What do you think will happen to her?"

"I don't know. I don't know anything. Hopefully, she's in seclusion, and then they send her back to our room. I hope they don't do whatever they did to Judy." The thought is terrifying.

All of us are one mistake away from no longer being ourselves.

Quiet hour is even more quiet than usual.

Judy 1 lies in her bed, as she was told to.

Mary sits up and stares.

I find myself staring into space as well.

"Well, now what?" says the little girl. She's standing at the foot of the bed. Her usual smile is replaced by a grim expression.

I sigh. "I have no idea." I'm tired. I didn't sleep much last night, and I think the sleep I did get was on the concrete floor.

"You have to do something. You know that." She's insistent now, looking at me intently.

"I don't even know what to do next. I know that what's going on here is wrong, but I'm literally in this place because I'm crazy. Who is going to believe me? Who would I even begin to try to tell?" I put my head in my hands.

Being sober now, I understand how dire our situation here is.

But I don't have any idea who I could turn to in an attempt to fix it.

"What about your brother?" Mary's voice is quiet from across the room.

I look up, and she's looking at me. "What?" I ask her.

"Your brother. You wrote about him on your notecard. I'm sorry that I snooped, but I was really curious what kind of notes you were taking." She looks down, ashamed to have admitted that she looked at my personal effects.

For a minute, I feel violated, but then I realize she's right. I don't remember Vic, but I know he exists because of the cards. He must visit. Maybe he's coming soon? I only have a foggy recollection of the visitation room, but maybe it's private enough for me to get him the message.

"That's a terrific idea," I tell Mary. "It can't be too long before he's going to visit again."

She smiles, glad to have helped me. It helps her, too.

An orderly opens the door. "Activity time! Moren, Visitor!" He shuts the door behind him.

Mary and I look at each other. "That's timely," she says, smiling.

I shuffle into the visitors' lounge. Most of the tables are empty, but one in the corner has guests, but no visitors.

I was expecting a man, but it's a couple; a man and a woman. They're older, late fifties, maybe early sixties.

The man looks up and sees me. His eyes go wide. "Nadia! Come here! We're so happy to see you." He stands, giving me an awkward hug before we sit.

As I adjust to the soft lighting and comfortable chair, I also adjust my expectations for this visit.

I look up. My breath catches in my chest.

The woman sitting in front of me is the woman from my sketch. I've sketched her twice now. Her blonde hair is perfectly styled, and a pair of Jackie O sunglasses rests on top of her head. Her makeup is muted, demure. She has a guilty look on her face, and she has trouble making eye contact.

Who is she?

The man sitting next to her looks tired, worn down. He's gruff-looking. Slightly heavy. Stubble a few days old. They make an odd pair, and the energy between them is restless, like they don't belong here.

When nobody speaks, I start. "Hi."

"Hello," they say at the same time, though it sounds discordant.

"I'm sorry, but I don't have much memory of before I came here. Both of you look familiar, but I can't say that I remember either of you." I look down, ashamed. I know this isn't really my own fault, but I can imagine how shocking it must be to hear those words coming from someone you love.

The woman sucks in air, and her eyes fill with tears, though she dabs at them with a hankie she has at the ready, like she was expecting to cry. "Oh, Nadia, honey. I'm your mom." She looks at the man sitting beside her. "This is your dad." She cries softly, dabbing at her tears with the hankie.

I reach out and put a hand over hers. "It's going to be okay. It is. You don't need to cry."

She looks up, then over to my dad. "She seems more aware than Vic made her sound."

I have to suppress an eye-roll. Imagine talking about someone as if they're not sitting in front of you.

I want to tell them that I've stopped taking my meds, but I don't know if I can trust them.

I don't know if I can trust Vic either. I need to feel my parents out to see where this visit is going.

"I am more aware than when Vic was here last. I actually don't remember seeing him."

Mom looks up, shocked. "You don't remember him being here just a few days ago?"

"No," I tell her. "I know he was here, because I've been doing my best to keep notes of what's been going on, but I don't have any memory of meeting with him."

She looks again at my dad, and he finally speaks. His voice is deep and slightly hoarse. "What kind of notes are you keeping?" He seems very interested.

I need to tread lightly. I know someone put me here, and I'm not sure who I can trust. "Just notes of my daily activities. It's helped me to remember, cut through the fog of my medication. They've been helping, for sure."

Dad sits back in his chair, processing the information. My mom blows her nose, and tears continue to spill down her face.

"Maybe you should come home," Mom says. "I'm really thinking this was a huge mis—"

Dad cuts her off. "Honey." He looks at her hard. "This is important. It's important that she gets well. We can't just pull her out of here. There's too much at stake." He turns to me. "Nadia, getting healthy is your first and only priority. Once we know you're well, we'll take you home." He sits back in the chair as if that conversation is settled now.

Mom's eyes are wide, and she looks like he just slapped her. "Hank, are you serious? You can't really expect her to stay here. She doesn't even know who we are. She doesn't even know *me*! This really feels like a situation where she could get better at *home*." She places a strange emphasis on the last word.

I look at her, then at him. I decide based on what I've learned, I'm going to try to make my case.

I lean in and whisper, "Bad things happen here." I look at the nurse and orderlies who are chaperoning the room, but they aren't paying attention. "A friend of mine had some sort of surgery yesterday, and she's not the same now. It's like she's flat; her entire personality is gone. I'm scared."

Mom's face drains of color, and I can see that this has even affected my dad. Little beads of sweat have popped up on his brow.

I think I'm having an effect. "They over-medicate us to keep us foggy and compliant. If you show too much emotion, even frustration for being so drugged up, they'll administer shock treatment. I've had it done. I don't remember it, but the doc recaps it whenever he does his rounds." I look over, and the nurse seems to be listening in. I speak up.

"And they added an art table with colored pencils and markers! They have coloring pages, as well as blank paper. I've found out I'm quite the artist. I have a talent for drawing faces!" I beam at them and glance back at the nurse.

She seems to have lost interest.

All the blood has drained from Mom's face. Dad also looks slightly sick.

"I… I had no idea," he stutters. "We'll get this fixed right away. Give me a couple of days to get the paperwork straightened out, but we'll pull you out of here. You can't stay. Especially not in this condition."

What a weird thing to say. Isn't my condition the reason I'm here to begin with?

"A couple of days? Are you crazy?" Mom is looking at him as if he's the one who belongs in an institution. "She needs to come home *now*."

He sighs as he turns to her. "Doreen, you can't just walk out of a facility with a patient. There is paperwork and red tape to cut through. I will straighten it out as quickly as possible. I promise."

I let out my breath. "Thank you," I tell them. "Thank you so much. You have no idea how relieving that is. A few days is nothing; I can handle that."

Mom has tears pouring down her face. The hankie is not nearly enough reinforcement.

Dad looks gray. I can tell this is not how he wanted or expected this visit to go.

Our time is nearly up, so I stand and give each of them a long hug. "I love you," I tell them.

"I love you too, honey. I'm so sorry." Mom is still beside herself, and I feel bad for bringing this on her.

Dad grumbles out an "I love you too," but it feels forced and awkward. "I'll be in touch soon."

I'm so relieved to be getting out of here.

Fifteen

Dinner is just Betty, Mary, and me again. Judy 1 may be back to her normal routine by tomorrow, but I don't know if she'll sit with us or have anything to contribute to the conversation.

I tell Betty all about my meeting with my parents and how they're going to get me released and take me home. She seems happy for me, but sad. I know how badly she wants to get out of here, too.

"How did your visit with your husband go?" I ask her.

She looks grim. "It went okay. We talked for a while, and he said he's going to ask about bringing me home, but I got a weird feeling. I don't know." Her eyes fill up, but the tears don't fall.

"I'm sorry, Betty." I'm not sure what else to say. I don't think there is anything I can offer to make her feel better.

Mary smiles at me. "I'm glad you're going home."

"Thanks," I say. "I'm glad too."

Betty looks over at Mary, but then looks away. I hope it didn't hurt her further.

I walk into room 108 and see that the Judys are both back now. Mary comes in behind me and takes the normal route to her bed.

Judy 1 appears to be sleeping. Judy 2 is lying in bed, looking up at the ceiling.

I tentatively approach my bed and sit, facing her. "Judy?" It's a question.

She looks in my direction but has trouble focusing on me. "What?"

As she turns, I can see the singed hair at her temples. She's still in a hospital gown, and there's an almost… chemical smell emanating from her.

"Are you okay?" It hurts. These two women don't deserve to be here, having their lives stripped from them.

She gives me a tired smile. "I'm okay. Slight headache, but I'll be fine." She looks over to Judy 1. "She seems sleepy today. Is she okay?"

I realize with horror that she doesn't remember what happened to Judy 1. It's inhumane of the doctors and nurses to put her back in here now. It's like they're trying to provoke her so they can take her away again.

I decide not to stir the pot tonight and let Judy 2 rest. "Yeah, she seems fine. She's been tired the last couple of days."

Judy 2 nods, accepting this information.

The nurse comes in, and rounds are administered. Judy 1 wakes briefly for her medication but goes right back to sleep. Judy 2 is right behind her.

It's just Mary and me now. Well, the little girl, too. She's sitting in the empty bed next to me, back against the wall. She doesn't talk as much these days, now that I'm remembering most of the time on my own.

I take out my notecard and add:

Mom and Dad Visit – surgeries, overmedication. Taking me home.

I smile. The relief is palpable, knowing that I'm getting out of this place. It's like there's a light at the end of this crazy tunnel. And even though I'm definitely still mentally unwell, I know that I'll do better somewhere that punishment doesn't mean stripping your very essence away.

The little girl looks at me and smiles. "I'm glad that you're getting out. Even if you didn't remember it all."

She's right. There's still so much that I don't know about my life, about my past. But I can continue figuring it all out, outside of here. I don't need to be behind these walls to keep making progress.

"So am I. I just wish I could help Mary and the Judys, too. It's so dangerous. Nobody belongs here." I lay back on my pillow. Within minutes, I'm asleep. Dreaming of what life will be like outside these walls.

I wake late into the night.

Sitting up, I see Mary is awake too.

"It's the screams again," Mary tells me. She's clutching at her thin blanket as if it will protect her from the horrors of this place.

Then I hear them drifting down the hall. The sound sends a chill up my spine. What I witnessed the other night was wrong. I may not have known exactly what they were doing, but I know they wait until they think everyone is asleep for a reason.

I think again of the "Research Studies" filing cabinet. I can't shake the feeling that there's information in those files that may be helpful to the women here if it got out.

If I were braver, there could be value in finding out what's stored in there. But I'm not brave. I'm too close to getting out myself to put it on the line.

I know that makes me a coward.

Mary is looking at me, and it feels eerie. Like she knows what I'm thinking and is disappointed.

I get up and walk to the door. I tell myself that if it's not locked, I'll go see what I can see. Maybe the nurses' station is unoccupied again.

I put my hand on the handle. I'm terrified. Everything in me hopes that it doesn't turn.

It doesn't.

I let out a sigh and relax, before walking back to my bed.

Mary is still looking at me.

I feel like I failed. But I'm relieved that I did.

I wake the next day for rounds. Mary is lying in her bed, looking at the ceiling. Judy 1 is sitting up with a placid look on her face. Judy 2 stirs and sits up. She instinctively reaches for Judy 1's hand and grasps it. Judy 1 allows it, but continues to face forward. She doesn't even acknowledge Judy 2.

Judy 2's face is confused. "Judy, what's wrong?"

Judy 1 turns slowly to look at her. "Nothing, I'm fine." She gives her that smile that doesn't reach her eyes. It's haunting to watch a woman I once knew operating as a ghost of herself.

Judy 2 is still foggy from extra meds and her procedure. "You don't seem fine. What's wrong?" She rubs her eyes and tries to focus on Judy 1's face.

I feel very sorry for her. I can't even imagine having to learn all over again that something terrible happened to someone you love. It was hard enough to watch the first time. I'm worried about what will happen this time.

The nurse enters at that moment, and Judy 2 releases Judy 1's hand.

I'm grateful the nurse showed up when she did.

That's a first.

Rounds are administered, and the four of us shuffle off to breakfast.

Betty is already waiting, picking at her powdered eggs and toast. She sees the four of us coming, and her eyes open wider. When we sit, she isn't sure what to say. She looks to me to begin, possibly afraid of saying the wrong thing.

I don't know what to say either. I feel a distance between myself and these other women now. It's like I've been marked for release, and they as sheep for slaughter.

I don't want to talk about going home; it feels like bragging. But I don't know how else to relate to them.

"Judy and Judy, I know you weren't around yesterday, but my parents came to visit, and they're going to take me home. They're finalizing the paperwork. Even as crazy as I am, telling them about this place was enough to get them to pull me out." I smile shyly. It still feels wrong to say out loud, but I'm not even sure what else we would talk about.

Judy 2 looks up from her eggs and snorts. "Yeah, good luck with that. They don't let us out."

I'm glad to see that whatever happened to her, her personality is still intact. Even if her full memory of this last week doesn't seem to be.

"I guess that's possible. But knowing I have people on the outside working to get me out gives me some hope," I tell her.

Judy 2 realizes how rude her statement was. She looks at Judy 1, who would normally have chastised her for being callous.

Judy 1 is slowly chewing her eggs, staring at nothing. She doesn't interject or add to the conversation. It's as if she doesn't hear what's going on around her.

"What's with you today?" Judy 2 says gruffly, grabbing Judy 1's face in her hand and turning her head towards her. "Why are you so out of it?"

I hear Betty gasp. She hadn't anticipated this turn of events.

Judy 1 gives her a smile. "I'm fine, thank you."

Judy 2's hand drops from her face, and I can see the realization dawning, feel the horror building inside her.

It's palpable.

"Jesus Christ," she whispers, dropping her fork. "They did this because of me." Putting her head in her hands, I see her shoulders start to heave.

A nurse approaches at that moment. "Everything alright here, ladies?" She looks at each face as if she's trying to read what's going on.

Judy 2 pops up with a fake smile on her face. "Just fine," she says, a little too brightly. The tears in her eyes don't fall, but they're visible.

The nurse looks at her a moment, and she puts her head down and shovels eggs into her mouth. The nurse nods and makes a note on her clipboard, then moves on.

I look around at these women whom I've grown to care for. They're trapped here, like caged birds.

My heart clenches. I hate to leave them behind, but if there's a way out, I can't stay for them.

This place takes the humanity from all of us, with or without procedures.

Sixteen

After nurses' rounds, I add my pill to the cup under my mattress. It's starting to fill up. Every time I add a pill, it feels like I'm adding moments back to my life. Moments I would otherwise have completely forgotten.

I feel a pang as I think about my unknown past. I know I have parents and a brother, but are there other people I care about? People who care about me? I've been so drug-addled for months that I don't even know if anyone else has come to visit.

Thinking rationally, I know I'm here for my psychosis. So, I probably don't have a husband or kids in my life. But what if something happened to make me this way, and there are other people out there missing me?

My eyes fill slightly as I think about the mystery relationships I have outside of Ravensbrook. I want so badly to know who I was. Who I am.

Now that I'm completely clear of the drugs, the shakiness and agitation have died down. I look at the bed next to me. The little girl is doing a crossword puzzle. She looks up and smiles at me. I smile back. The psychosis is still here, but the aggression is not.

I shuffle out to OT, wondering what our activity for the day is. The room is full of arts and crafts supplies. Wicker strips for basket weaving, felt and ribbon scraps, paints, pipe cleaners, and just about anything else you could think of.

It's a relaxing couple of hours, and I've gotten good at keeping my projects right in the middle of the pack. I don't do too well, and I don't do too poorly. Faking fogginess is now a talent of mine. I even drew a few sketches to bring back with me. Mom and Dad, Mary, the little girl.

Nurse Delaney stops by right before time is up. "Nadia, these are beautiful! It's nice that you've found a talent that you enjoy. Who are they?" she points to the picture of my parents.

Is it me? Or is her hand shaking?

"My mom and dad. They came to visit… I don't remember when," I tell her. I need to keep up the charade until I'm out of here.

"Oh." For a moment, she seems to hesitate. "That's wonderful, hon. And these other two?"

I can't tell her the little girl is a figment of my imagination. "Oh, that's my niece. The other is my roommate, Mary."

She looks confused for a moment, and then recognition hits. "Oh, right. Your fourth roommate. I forget about her, she's so quiet." She laughs at herself.

I smile. Mary does stay quiet and minds her own business.

Nurse Delaney turns to the group, smiling broadly. "Okay, everyone! Time for lunch!" She starts herding everyone out into the hallway.

My thought from breakfast echoes in my head.

Sheep for slaughter.

Lunch is quiet. Nobody knows what to say. Betty didn't even sit with us, though I don't see her sitting elsewhere either. I hope she's okay and that nothing happened to her.

Judy 1 smiles demurely if you make eye contact, but doesn't have anything to say anymore. The most you'll get out of her is "I'm fine" or "Oh, that's nice." Her whole life has been washed away, replaced by a replica of the woman we once knew, but without her depth.

Judy 2 is a wreck, but does her best to stay calm. I'm sure the meds help; she seems very foggy herself now. She doesn't look up from her plate, just stares into her soup.

A nurse comes by and shovels some into Judy 2's mouth. She obliges and swallows, but doesn't pick the spoon up to feed herself.

"Well, this is depressing," Mary says to me quietly.

The Judys don't even look up. We may as well be sitting here alone.

"Yeah," I whisper. I don't think they're listening, but I don't want to talk about them like they aren't here, and the conversation fizzles out.

Quiet time is just that. The silence is so loud I can hear my own heart beating. I take my notes out and go through them for the hundredth time. I'll be glad when I'm out of here and can keep notes in a real notebook while I recover my memory.

I wonder again about the yellow house with the periwinkle shutters.

Is it my house? Do my parents and I live there? Is it Vic's place? What is my connection to it?

Do I have pets? I think I'd like to have a dog, if I don't. If I do live alone, a dog would be good company.

I probably don't live alone, not in my condition.

I spend the time dreaming of what I'll be like when I'm free of Ravensbrook. Who will I be when the threat of having my life stripped away is removed?

Right now, I have no answers. But soon I will.

The rest of the day and night slides by, and I watch, scene by scene, as if it's happening to someone else. I've mentally checked out of here, and now I'm just waiting for them to call my number so I can hop on the first train out.

The next morning begins, and it's like watching a rerun of a show that I've seen a million times. Mary is quiet, the Judys are complacent and medically contained. Breakfast, OT, and lunch pass at record speed.

I have a feeling that today is the day things are going to change. There's an energy in me that has been missing up to this point. I think even the little girl can feel it. She seems jumpy, too. Full of anticipation, like it's the first day of school.

She's sitting on the bed next to me with a coloring book, heavily invested in filling in a day at the beach. Noticing me looking, she turns. "What?"

"You've been quiet lately." I'm curious why.

She thinks for a moment. "Yes. I'm here to help you remember, but you're doing it on your own." She turns back to her page and continues coloring.

"I don't remember everything, though."

Glancing up, she sets her crayon down. "You don't. But you don't need reminders anymore."

She's right. I've created a system to remind me. It would be redundant if she did too.

"There is one thing, though." She looks at me intently, as if she's checking that I'm listening. "I told you that you have to do something. You ignored me."

"What could I possibly do?" I sigh. She just called me out in a way I wasn't ready for. I feel like shit knowing that even though I'm leaving, everyone else has to stay. "Do you want me to play hero? I don't understand. I'm just a mentally damaged woman trying to survive. How am I supposed to save everyone else?" I'm frustrated and a little hurt. I know she's part of my own mind, and that her words are just my own guilt. Survivor's guilt. But it still stings to have a child look at you like you could or should be doing more.

"There is more you could do." She turns her attention fully back to coloring, as if the conversation is over.

"Do you ever stop?" I blurt out. "Talking in riddles?"

She grins at her paper and doesn't look up.

"Will you be gone when I leave this place?"

Her crayon stops, hovering over the image. "I don't know, do you want me to?"

I don't answer.

Seventeen

"Activity Room! Moren, visitor!" The orderly slams the door behind him.

Visitor. Did Mom and Dad come back to get me? Would they be considered 'visitors' if they had? Probably not. Maybe they're here to give me an update on how my release is going. Either way, I'm glad to see the face of someone from the outside world. A world that I'm going to be a part of again, very soon.

I shuffle down to the visitors' lounge and open the door. Looking around, I deflate a little when I don't see my parents sitting at any of the tables. As the door shuts behind me, a man sitting to my right stands up, making eye contact.

"Vic?" I say. I don't remember him at all, but it's my best guess based on what I know.

He starts slightly. "You remember me? Last time you didn't." There's a look of relief in his eyes.

"Well, not exactly." I approach and sit down across from him in the comfy chair. "I don't remember our last visit, but I've been keeping notes. It was an educated guess." I chuckle.

He doesn't. His smile of relief has disappeared.

I look at him, study him for a moment. He's handsome. His dark hair and the gold rim around his eyes seem to play off each other. I wonder briefly what color my own eyes are.

Finally, I speak.

"Mom and Dad visited me a couple of days ago." I lower my voice, unsure how much the nurses know. The less, the better. "I told them what's been going on here, and they said they're going to get me out." I sit back in the chair, relaxed in a way I haven't felt in a very long time.

Vic rubs the back of his neck with his hand, looking uncomfortable. "Yeah, about that. It's one of the reasons I'm here, besides checking on you." He looks at me, trying to gauge how much information I've gotten from that sentence, how aware I am. "You seem different this time. More alert. Did something change? You were like a freaking zombie last time. I don't even think you were paying attention." He leans forward.

I smile, keeping my voice low. "I've been skipping meds. It's actually not that hard, the nurses are so busy that they don't do a thorough job checking. I spent the last couple of months in such a haze that I still have no memory of my life before coming here, but I want to put that behind me. I'm trying to stay as sober as possible, so I can regain my memory. It's been about a week, and I feel a lot better than I did." I think about what he just told me, then add. "Are you here to take me home?"

He pushes back in his chair and lets out a long sigh, crossing his arms. "There's been some issues with getting the paperwork finalized."

Wait. What does he mean? "The paperwork? What paperwork?" My chest tightens.

He breaks eye contact and looks at the floor. "Your last name, Moran, was misspelled on your intake form. They spelled it Moren. It's a stupid little clerical issue, but there are now legal hoops that we have to jump through to prove that you are Nadia Moran, not Nadia Moren. It's a bureaucratic nightmare. The institute won't even confirm you exist until they get confirmation from the State."

I get the feeling that he was almost hoping I wasn't going to remember this conversation. "What does that mean? How long will it take to fix it so I can get out of here?"

I can feel panic rising in my chest. I have to swallow it, remain calm. The last thing I need to do is to end up dosed because I got upset.

I whisper again, "You don't understand how bad it is. I've watched women who did nothing wrong, end up with…" I look toward the nurse and orderlies who are on watch. They're busy chatting. "…surgeries," I mouth the last word, hoping he gets it. "They aren't who they were. It's terrifying."

Vic's eyes go wide. "Are you serious?" He can't find the words to describe the horror that is playing across his face like a movie at a drive-in theater.

He runs his fingers through his messy hair. I can see the wheels turning in his head, trying to think of a way out of this. He comes up blank.

"I'm so sorry, Nadia." He grabs my hand and holds it. "I promise, I'm doing everything I can. Mom and Dad are doing everything in their power to resolve this. I'm not going to let this happen to you."

My body feels numb. How could this happen? I am so close to being free of this hellscape. I thought I was just biding my time, that I'd be free today or tomorrow.

"Is there any other way?" I ask him. My eyes plead with him to fix this, to make it better, to take me home.

He sits back, looking angry, scared, and helpless. Then, I watch as an idea dawns on him. "Nadia," he whispers. "You said 'surgeries.' What kind of surgeries? Do they seem…" Now it's his turn to look up at the nurse and orderlies. "… legal?"

I'm stunned. I have no idea what's legal and what isn't. "How would I know? I didn't even realize they've been calling me by the wrong name." My eyes fill with tears, but I can't, won't, let them fall.

Vic takes my hand again. "I'm sorry. I didn't mean to make you upset. I was just trying to think of another way to get you out of here."

I use my sleeve to wipe the tears away before our chaperones see me upset. "Is there a way for me to know? If what's going on is legal?" An idea is starting to form. I look down, and the little girl is sitting at my feet.

She smiles up at me. "I told you, there is more you could do."

I don't smile back. Instead, I look at Vic. "How would I know, and how do I prove it?"

He looks at me. He isn't smiling. "Nadia, please forget it. With everything that could happen, it's not worth it. I'm sorry I mentioned it. You are a dose of medication from forgetting that I exist again." He looks up to the nurse again, before whispering, "There is no possible way that you're going to unravel a crime ring, if that's what is happening here. Please, just lay low and we'll get the paperwork fixed as quickly as we can."

It's too late for that now. The little girl has been trying to tell me all along that I can't just save myself. She knew, even if I was too scared to recognize it. If I'm stuck here right now, I need to do what I can. For Mary, for the Judys, for Betty.

"Vic, what would I need? What kind of evidence?" The tears are gone now, and my mind is racing. My thoughts turn to the records room. *Research Studies. Patient Outcomes.*

Vic is silent; he looks grim. "Nadia, I…"

"What would I need, Vic?" I spoke too loudly, and the nurse's head swiveled as if I had screamed.

I plaster on my crooked smile and briefly make eye contact with her before turning my attention back to Vic. "I can't believe she turned seven!"

The nurse, satisfied that my outburst was excitement at something my brother told me, and not anger, turns back to flirting with one of the orderlies.

"Would copies of paperwork be enough? There's a records room just inside the nurses' station. I can start there." I am determined now. My panic has subsided and has been replaced by the certainty that this is bigger than just freeing myself. My mind is whirring now. Preparations need to be made. Carefully thought out. This isn't going to be a quick mission. It requires precision and a solid plan.

I look up again, and Vic is smiling at me.

"What?"

He sighs. "Nothing, it's just nice to see you feeling a little more yourself. You never were easy to talk out of something once you got it in your head." He readjusts in his chair. "If you can find something, anything, showing the institution is doing unapproved procedures, it would be helpful. That sounds easier than it probably is."

"How often are you able to visit? If I can get proof, how quickly can I get it to you?" The plan is trying to come together in my mind even as the thought is still solidifying.

"I can probably visit twice a week without suspicion, but more than that, and I'm going to get the side-eye. How are you planning to get them? Especially if you end up medicated again?"

He's right. All of this is going to require some thinking through, but right now I've got nothing but time. "Yeah, you're right. I'm going to have to find a way. When can you visit again?"

"Three days. I can come back in three days." He's looking at me, scrutinizing the details of my face. "Nadia, you need to be very careful. If we're dealing with what you think we're dealing with, this isn't going to be a walk in the park. It's dangerous. Your very life may depend on how invisible you can be."

I give him a small smile. "I've gotten very good at being invisible. Come back in three days, and we'll finalize the plan."

He looks tired and worried.

"Can I ask you something?" There's a question that has been rolling around in my head for days, and I need an answer.

"Anything," he says, squeezing my hand.

I feel a new pen slide between my fingers. Smiling, I bend down and tuck it into my slipper.

Sitting back up, I ask, "How did I end up here?" I want to understand the depth of my psychosis. To know how bad it really is. Knowing this answer feels like the first step in figuring out the rest.

He sighs. "You asked to be put here."

I'm shocked. "Really?" That wasn't the answer I was expecting.

He nods. "You insisted. Wouldn't take no for an answer. You had to 'make things right.'" He adds softly, "'A burden.' That's what you said," He looks up and makes eye contact, gauging how I'm taking this news.

"Oh." I'm not sure what else to say. Is trying to get out of here a mistake? If it was that important to me to be committed in the first place?

"For what it's worth, I never thought you belonged here. Letting you do this was a mistake."

"Thanks, Vic." That helps.

If I can't leave quietly, I'll unravel this place silently.

Eighteen

After dinner, I'm back in 108 to wind down before bedtime, but there is no relaxing now.

My mind is spinning, turning ideas over until they're smooth. Trying to find simple solutions to complicated problems.

I may have lost my memory, but I understand how long bureaucratic red tape can take to untangle. It could be months, if I'm lucky.

I need to find evidence of the horrors going on here as much for me as for everyone else. I don't want my fate to rest on a judge somewhere deciding if I actually exist.

The nurse comes in for the nightly routine. When she leaves, I store my latest pill and give the cup a little shake. It makes a pleasant rattling sound, all the missed pills jingling together a little tune.

A song of sanity.

An idea pops into my head. I write it down on my notecard.

A real plan is beginning to form, but I know it's going to take a lot of different pieces coming together at the right time.

I review my list of nurses, the ones who are always distracted or don't seem to care. There are about a dozen names. Plenty of opportunities to move my plan in the right direction.

Now I need to figure out their rotations.

As my mind turns over the ideas, a memory surfaces.

It's Mom. She's younger, maybe thirty or thirty-five.

I close my eyes and picture her face, trying to hold on to the image. Attempting to expand this fragment.

She's smiling and laughing. There's a board game set in front of us. She picks up the dice and gives them a good shake in her fists, then lets them go. They go skittering across the board and land.

"I win!" She stands up and pushes her chair back from the table, doing a silly celebratory dance. Then she runs around to the other side and grabs me, kissing my face and tickling me.

I'm laughing, but I'm mad that she won.

She continues tickling me. "Don't be a poor sport, Nadia. You have to learn to lose too."

I stomp my foot. "I hate losing."

Mom hugs me. "Well, I love you anyway."

The memory fades, and I open my eyes, half expecting to see Mom's face in front of me, the woodgrain of the kitchen table, and the game still in sight.

All I see is the cold sterility of the concrete walls of the asylum. It's a stark contrast to the warmth of my childhood kitchen.

Despite the somberness of this room and how sterile and suffocating the institution feels, there's a warmth inside me now that I want more of.

I remember something from my past.

I wake in complete darkness.

Listening for a moment, I don't hear anything unusual. I look around, and the Judys and Mary are all still asleep.

What woke me?

Getting out of bed, I move toward the door and peer into the hallway. Darkness. No movement, no sound.

I go back to bed and sit with the stillness. I'm not tired. My brain may just be too worked up to keep sleeping.

It's been an interesting twenty-four hours, to say the least. Thinking I was leaving, realizing I wasn't, and then having an actual pre-Ravensbrook memory is quite a day.

I think again of the kitchen, the board game, and Mom's happy dance.

I smile, playing it over and over again in my mind. Being able to remember that hug is nearly as good as getting one.

I frown. I really wish I had this memory before she came to visit. It paints the whole exchange in a new light. Her distress at seeing me and hearing about what had been going on feels more genuine now.

I know she loved me. Loves me.

I sit in the dark for a few more moments, replaying the new memory, contrasting it with the visit from my parents.

Dad wasn't part of the memory, just Mom and me.

I pick apart both scenes, trying to peer into the cracks. Like having a tooth removed, but still pressing your tongue into the space that's left behind.

I come up empty. There's nothing else that my mind wants to add to the memory. No new clues as to who I was, who I am.

I get out of bed again and pace back and forth. Door to bed, bed back to door. I feel restless. For months, I didn't mind being stuck in a small room most of the time, but now it's different. Being aware and lucid changes everything. I'm slowly going stir-crazy.

A thought occurs to me. I walk over and check the door handle.

It's unlocked.

My heart beats faster. What do I have to gain? There are no screams tonight. Is there a benefit to seeing what's going on down the hall?

I decide it's worth a shot.

Opening the door, I tiptoe out into the hall. I listen, but I can't hear anything over the sound of the blood rushing in my head. I close my eyes and take a minute to breathe, calming myself.

When I open them, I can see better. My heart still beats fast, but it has steadied.

I take small, quiet steps toward the nurses' station. As I approach, I can hear noises long before I can see anything. The smell of coffee drifts down the hall. It's a nice change from the antiseptics and alcohol.

There's a song playing faintly in the background. It sounds familiar, but I can't place it.

You can check out any time you like, but you can never leave.

I almost laugh, but catch myself. Isn't that fitting?

I get a brief glimpse of being in a car, wind in my hair and warmth on my skin, but it passes.

I continue sneaking towards the nurses' station, back pressed to the wall. There's a column that stands right before it, and I make my way up to it and stand still, listening.

A nurse hums. I can hear the scratching sound of pencils as they complete today's paperwork, the rustling of the sheets as they're shuffled around.

One of the nurses speaks. "I'm glad there are no surgeries tonight. They wear on me. It's a nice break to just have paperwork to complete."

The other voice sounds familiar. Nurse Delaney, maybe. "I don't mind surgery. I think what's happening here is cutting-edge, and it's exciting to be able to see it happening from the ground floor. Someday, what we're doing here is going to be mainstream and help a lot of people." Her pencil continues scratching the paper, and I hear her start to hum the chorus of the song on the radio.

The other nurse audibly shudders. "I don't like it one bit. Whether it's groundbreaking or not, a lot of it feels wrong."

The familiar voice speaks again. "You may want to find a different institute, then. Sure, there are some sacrifices, but on the whole it's for the greater good."

I peek around the corner briefly. The familiar voice is Nurse Delaney.

Hearing this conversation gives me a shiver down my spine. Just as I'm about to start my tiptoe back to 108, I hear the other nurse yell, "Hey! What do you think you're doing?"

I freeze, flattening against the wall and squeezing my eyes shut, mentally preparing to act like I'm sleepwalking. I don't think that the nurses will buy it, especially Delaney.

But I have to try.

"You know we're not supposed to drink, especially on the night shift! Are you trying to get all of us fired?" She's laughing now.

I open my eyes and peek around the corner again. An orderly is pouring something from a flask into his cup of coffee and grinning. "Come on, we have to liven it up a little. How else do you stay awake all night?"

I don't stick around to find out her answer. I run as silently as possible back to 108, making sure to shut the door behind me just as quietly. Leaping into bed, I pull the covers over my head and try to steady my breathing and still my racing heart.

Nobody follows.

That was a close call.

I need to be more careful.

Taking out my notecard, I add:

Delaney – Okay with surgeries
Orderly(ies) – Drink at night

This is the second time I've noticed my door being unlocked. I'm going to have to start checking every night. It probably happens more than I realize. I need to gather as much information as I can.

It will help in the long run with gathering evidence.

Nineteen

The next morning, I'm tired. I had lain awake until the sky started to lighten, and only then fell back asleep.

All day, I pay extra attention. To the nurses, the orderlies. To the other patients. I listen in on every conversation, especially the ones people try to hide.

I keep up my foggy, near-incoherent act, but underneath, I'm always listening. Watching which orderlies enjoy the gruesome parts of their jobs and which nurses take out their frustrations on patients. Whose smiles are fake and whose stories are overly cheerful.

I'm a sponge, soaking up any and all information I can get my hands on now.

I long ago filled up my first three cards, and I have a whole piece of paper, front and back, that I took from the art table in the activity room.

The list continues to grow as I note which nurses are working today and which shifts they are on. I plan to track it and create a system.

I know which nurses pay the least attention.

Now I need their schedules.

My plan is still solidifying, but I know the basics. I need proof of what is causing the screams. Getting that proof isn't going to be easy. It's going to take every brain cell I have and a whole lot of luck to get it done.

At dinner, I'm quietly running through my options while watching the staff. I'm so in my own head, I don't realize that Betty is talking to me.

"Hello? Earth to Nadia?" She's looking at me intently. Even Mary has taken a break from staring into space to smirk at me for not paying attention.

"Sorry, just in my own head. What did you say?" I put down my fork to give her my undivided attention.

"I asked if there was any news about you getting out." She looks melancholy.

"Oh, well… my brother came to visit yesterday, and there's been a snag on the paperwork side of things. Apparently, they spelled my name wrong on the intake form." I shrug.

Betty is looking at me wide-eyed. "Are you serious? Your family wants to pull you out, and they can't?"

I nod. "Yup. Sounds like it."

She scrunches up her face. "Doesn't that seem… weird?"

I freeze. "What do you mean, weird?"

She sighs. "It's probably nothing, but doesn't it just feel like this is all a big racket? Like, these are the people who brought you here, but they can't get you out?"

"Yeah, it does seem weird. But you know how it goes with paperwork. A clerical error can take a while to straighten out."

Betty shrugs and goes back to her food, but the question stays with me.

My parents, Vic… They wouldn't lie to me, would they?

For the first time, I find myself questioning what I've been told.

Is it possible that it's not the truth?

After evening rounds and lights out, I get out of bed and start pacing the floor. Mary and Judy 1 don't acknowledge me, but Judy 2 seems agitated.

"Are you going to go to bed, or just walk around all night?" The bags under her eyes make her look years older than just a week ago. Sitting up in bed, she looks like a small child who is fighting her nightly routine. Mouth set in a stubborn line, eyes angry, covers half pulled up her torso.

"Sorry, Judy. I'm not trying to disturb you. I'm just having a hard time sleeping these days." I go back to sit on the edge of the bed.

"Yeah, well, that makes two of us." She lies back and stares at the ceiling.

"Are you okay? You've been so quiet lately. It's not like you."

She sits up and looks at me hard. "Are you serious? No, of course I'm not okay. Look at what they did to her." She points to Judy 1, who is half asleep. Judy 1 sees, but nobody speaks to her, so she ignores it.

Delaney's words from the night before echo in my head.

For the greater good.

"Yeah, I know. It's terrible. This place does awful things to people who don't deserve it."

"You're damn right they do. The worst part is that it's all my fault. I caused this. Because of me, they took her away. Maybe not physically, sure, she's lying right here. But it's not Judy anymore. It's like they replaced her with a Judy doll." Judy 2 cries silent tears, mourning the woman lying next to her. "I'm going to ask for a transfer tomorrow. I can't be in this room, watching her waste away. I know I'm a coward, but it's too hard."

"I don't think that makes you a coward," I say quietly. "I think it makes you human."

We're both silent.

Judy 2 lies down and pulls her blanket back up. "Goodnight, Nadia."

"Goodnight, Judy."

I lay awake late into the night, thinking about Vic, Betty, the Judys, and my parents. Life is complicated, no matter who you are. No matter where you are. But in this place, it's doubly so. Your very existence depends on others, and it can be taken away from you on the whim of a nurse or orderly.

Judy 2 fell asleep long ago, so I get up and pace the room. Back and forth, back and forth. I try the doorknob, but it doesn't turn.

I hadn't expected it to; Delaney did our rounds tonight.

The days are all starting to blur together, and the nights are long. I have a hard time relaxing enough to fall asleep.

Since the childhood memory of Mom surfaced, I've spent a lot of time trying to uncover others. When I'm not checking the nurses' schedules or eavesdropping, I'm thinking about the yellow house, Vic, and Mom and Dad.

The memory of Mom seemed to come out of nowhere when I was thinking about something else. I figure if I keep thinking, eventually new memories will surface.

At least, I hope they will.

I awake the next morning to a drizzly, gray day. The light that filters through the windows shines murky onto the concrete, casting a fog-like gloom.

I'm drowsy. I stayed up late into the night, staring at the ceiling and trying to rein in memories.

Occasionally, I'd get a flash of one: a scent, a texture, a quick visual, but then it was gone again.

I'm so tired I don't even have to pretend to be foggy for morning rounds. I briefly hear Judy 2 ask the nurse about changing rooms, and she tells her to talk to the charge nurse.

I'll be sad to see Judy 2 go, but I understand why she can't stay. I can't imagine how brutal it must be to see someone you love as a shell of themselves every single day.

We all shuffle off to breakfast, sitting down for the usual meal in our usual spot.

Mary seems restless today, like she can't sit still. She doesn't speak, but there's an energy to her that I'm not used to seeing.

We eat mostly in silence, with Betty and Judy 2 making small talk to break up the awkwardness.

Judy 2 finishes eating and gets up from the table to find the charge nurse.

I watch her locate the nurse with the stripe on her cap, about thirty feet away. She walks over and waits patiently for her attention. She stands calmly, just behind her, as she finishes up with another patient.

When the nurse turns around, Judy begins speaking. From this distance, I can't hear the conversation over the din of the dining room, but I watch as Judy's face changes. From calm, to shocked, to angry. Her shoulders stiffen, and her fists clench.

Don't do it, Judy. Don't explode. Especially here, so publicly.

Judy doesn't heed my silent advice. She picks up a plastic fork from the nearest table and lunges at the nurse with it, stabbing at her. The fork breaks on the collar of the nurse's dress and does no damage.

Three orderlies are restraining Judy before the charge nurse has time to react. Within thirty seconds, Judy is down, and the orderlies are dragging her out of the dining room.

It all happened so fast. Within two minutes, Judy got up from our table and was then dragged away, limp, by the orderlies.

I wonder how many times in the past I've seen this very scenario play out, and I didn't even react. I can't imagine just sitting here, eating powdered eggs, wondering what the nurses' uniform feels like, while women are dragged away into the unknown.

But it happens. I just witnessed it. None of the other patients even seemed to notice, aside from Betty and Mary.

Judy 1 didn't even react.

A line from Dante's *Inferno* begins to whirl around inside my head. It's stuck there, like a song you want to forget but won't go away.

Abandon all hope, ye who enter here.

Twenty

Back in 108, we make it through rounds and wait to be told it's time for OT.

Mary makes eye contact. "I don't know why, but I had a feeling that something was going to happen. That something was going to go wrong today."

I sigh. "I didn't have a good feeling when Judy got up to go speak to the nurse. Our needs aren't important to them. I was half expecting the fireworks." I lie down and stare at the ceiling. "You know, part of me misses being drugged into oblivion. At least I didn't really understand everything that was going on here the way I do now. I was less scared then."

"That's what I've been saying since the beginning. It's why I keep to myself and try not to cause problems. I don't want to be seen. Being seen means being noticed, and if you're noticed here, it's never for a good reason."

"What do you think will happen to Judy?" I ask softly, because I don't really want to know the answer.

"I don't know," Mary answers honestly. "But they aren't throwing her a party."

I hope that at least they move her to a new room, like she asked. It would have been easier on everyone if they had just listened in the first place.

The day wears monotonously on. It's amazing how much slower the clock seems to tick when you're aware of the horrors going on around you. In OT, someone has to be sedated for crying. At lunch, someone is dragged out screaming because they don't like broccoli.

I wonder how full the seclusion rooms are. How many of them are waiting for shock therapy, or worse?

By quiet time, I'm ready for a break from the madness.

Judy 1 is her new, complacent self. This is her normal now. She lies in bed resting unless someone speaks to her.

Mary is quiet today, too, almost as if she knows I don't want to talk.

With the stillness, I take the opportunity to nap. It's the only way to escape this place for a while.

I dream, but when I wake again, the memory drains away. I'm left with the knowledge that I did dream, but have no remnants of it.

The door opens, and an orderly announces activity time and that I have a visitor.

I smile. Maybe Vic has an update for me. As much as I've resigned myself to investigating in an attempt to help the other women here, it's still also for me. I can't say I would stay if Vic tells me I can be out in a few days.

It's cowardly, but every minute I spend here feels like a life sentence, probably because one slip-up could turn me into a completely different person.

I take my time, shuffling down the hall to the visitor's lounge. Opening the door, I spot Vic; he's managed to find a corner spot. It's semi-private, the furthest away from the chaperones.

"Hey," I say, sliding in across from him. I give him a small smile.

"Hi." He smiles back. "You remember me this time?"

"I do. I've been off my meds for a while now, and it's brought a lot of clarity."

"What about old memories? Do you remember anything from before?" He's sitting with his arms folded across his chest. He looks guarded.

"No, unfortunately not. Most of my memories are from the last week or two."

He deflates slightly. I think he was hoping that my memory would start to come back. "What do you mean, most?"

"Well, I did manage to recover a single childhood memory. It's of Mom. I was a kid, and we were playing a board game. That's it, though." I pause for a moment, then add, "But you weren't there."

He looks startled. "Oh, yeah. I'm a couple of years older than you. I must have been out with friends or something." Then he smiles. "I'm glad that even one memory has come back. Maybe that means it's just a matter of time until more do."

"I hope so. It's difficult not knowing who I am. Even who I was, before all of this." I gesture around the room. It's nearly as difficult as having to stay here.

Vic nods in agreement. "I can't imagine what that's like. You don't even remember me. It's hard to understand."

"So, do you have anything new to tell me?" I'm doubtful, but still hopeful.

He lets out a big sigh. "No. I wish I did, but everything is just stuck in the courts for now. We had to provide a ton of documentation: birth certificate, driver's license, the intake forms with the misspelled last name, among other things. It's a logistical nightmare." He looks up from examining the wood grain on the table. "What about you? I know you said you were forming a plan. Any luck there?"

In a hushed voice, I tell him about sneaking out of my room at night. About watching, listening, and creating the list and the nurses' schedules. About the stash of untaken pills under my mattress, and about the filing cabinets in the room adjacent to the nurses' station.

I know I'm taking a big risk by revealing my plan. Trusting anyone right now is a leap of faith.

I don't remember Vic, so I don't *know* that I can trust him, but some part of me feels it all the same. We have a connection, even if our past has been wiped from my memory.

I have a gut feeling he's not only my brother, but a true friend. Plus, I need his help for this to work.

"So, in short, yes. I have a plan, but I'm going to need to be smart and lucky."

Vic looks shocked that I have everything so fully thought out in just a few days. "You're taking this really seriously. That's good, because it will help in executing your plan, but please don't drive yourself crazy. I hope you're doing something other than planning." He catches himself, realizing what he just said. "I'm sorry, Nadia. Bad choice of words."

I look away and realize the little girl is playing cards by herself at a nearby table. She looks up at me and smiles, then goes back to her game. I wonder yet again if she's here forever, and if she's the reason I came here in the first place.

"Vic, can I ask you a difficult question?" I almost don't want to know the answer, but I need it.

"Of course, I already told you, ask me anything." He leans toward me.

"I… I don't have any… kids. Right?" I close my eyes and wince. I'm not really ready for his response.

"No, no, Nadia. You don't have any kids. You actually didn't have much of a personal life before coming here, either, if that makes you feel better. Wait, would that be better or worse?"

I breathe a huge sigh of relief, knowing that I'm not a mom and I didn't have anyone relying on me when I came here. "It's better. Thank you, Vic. That's a huge relief." My shoulders relax. "We still have about thirty minutes left. Can you tell me about life outside of here? It doesn't have to be about me; tell me about you. What you do for work, if you're married, what you do for fun. Being able to just listen may eventually help me unlock more memories, and that's what I'm after right now, outside of my plan."

I spend the rest of our visit listening to what is going on in Vic's life. He isn't married, though he's been with the same girlfriend for three years. No kids, though there was a near miss at one point. He works for the state, mostly paperwork and occasional meetings. He's three years older than I am, and growing up, we were inseparable. He took up golf for a while, and he enjoys all the walking, but he's terrible. Never makes par.

I laugh at his stories. It's nice to feel close to someone, even if my memory of him is still in the fog. When our time is up, he promises to come back in a few days.

I tell him that his visits make me feel alive in a way I haven't been in months. Talking to someone who isn't crazy is the best part of the week.

He laughs too. "Well, maybe not institutional, but probably not sane either."

I leave the visit with an optimism I haven't felt since being here.

Even being stuck for now, knowing I have a family outside who care about me means everything

Twenty-One

Dinner and night rounds fly by, and again it's dark and quiet in 108. I'm almost certain the door is unlocked. Nurse Trevany administered meds tonight; she always forgets to lock it behind her.

I get out of bed. Today, I decided to start exercising at night when everyone is asleep. I get on my hands and knees and start with pushups.

I can actually do a few. I didn't realize how strong I am. Moving on to sit-ups; I do fairly well with those, too.

Not bad for someone who hasn't done anything athletic in months. As I do another set of ten, I realize Mary is still awake.

"Are you going out there tonight?"

I start. I didn't know that she knew I'd snuck out before. "What?"

She smiles at me. "There are lots of nights I have trouble sleeping, too. Though I don't think you'd catch me exercising," She smirks.

I smile back. "I'll probably go. I'm trying to learn what I can."

Mary's face turns serious. "What are you looking for?"

I pause. I like Mary, and I don't think she'd tell anyone what I'm up to, but I don't trust anyone here.

She senses my hesitation. "It's okay, you don't have to tell me. I understand. But if you want to talk about it, I'm here. I won't tell anyone. I'm basically invisible."

I don't want to go into details with her. "I'm just looking for ways out."

She looks shocked. "Like, escape? Is that possible?"

"Oh, no. Nothing like that." Though, really, I hadn't thought of that. What if I did escape? Could they come after me?

No, that's not a real option.

I decide to give her a little information and see how she reacts. "I'm looking for proof that they're doing illegal things."

She nods. "Like the surgeries."

Now it's my turn to be shocked. "How did you know?"

"The screams. There's a reason they don't happen during the day."

She's right. It's not that hard to figure out when you aren't doped up on meds.

"If there's any way I can help, I will."

"Thanks, Mary. That means a lot." Maybe I do have an ally here after all.

I sneak out into the hallway and silently close the door.

Stepping as lightly as possible, I creep down the hall, trying my best to remain invisible.

In a moment, I quietly reach the nurses' station.

It's empty. The radio is off, coffee pot cold.

Strange. Where is everyone?

I continue creeping down the hall. I can hear movement from the procedure room.

Sneaking directly under the door, I peer in from the very bottom of the window.

A doctor, two nurses, and an orderly are standing around a patient on the table. There's a machine, attached to the wall by an electric cord, making loud humming sounds.

One of the nurse's shifts, and though I can't see the face of the woman on the table, I can see the doctor inserting what looks like small, square, metal strips under her skin by the temples.

I gasp and stagger back, appalled by what I just saw.

I need to go back and see what else happens, but I want to vomit and run away. Taking a few breaths, I creep back up to the window and peer in.

The doctor gestures to the nurse. She turns around and flips a switch on the machine, then a second.

The sound coming from the machine is part electric shock and part generator. It's an awful, ear-splitting sound.

Then they start. The screams. They're louder than I've ever heard and high-pitched enough that I'm surprised they don't break the glass of the window. The smell of burning hair and flesh fills the hallway.

I still don't know what's going on in there, but I've seen enough, and I need to get away. Stumbling back towards the nurses' station, I realize I'm going to be sick.

Ducking behind the counter, I find a trash can and retch what's left of my dinner into the pail.

I'm shaky, and I try to steady myself. A minute later, I begin to hobble back to 108. Hopefully, a janitor will be by soon, before the nurses notice my addition to their garbage.

I close the door to my room and lower myself slowly onto the bed. All the color must have drained from my face. I feel pale.

I don't remember sleeping, but I'm woken by an orderly announcing morning rounds. The stress of last night completely wore me out. I'm not exactly sure what I witnessed, but I know it wasn't right.

I need to find proof.

Nurse Delaney comes in to administer meds. She goes to Judy 1's bed first, and Judy complies with a smile. Delaney makes small talk when she works with patients. She really is the nicest nurse here. She makes a joke, and Judy smiles politely.

Delaney throws her head back and laughs, too big for this small room.

I can feel a memory trying to surface. It's pushing through the fog in my brain, crying out to escape. I get a flash of Delaney, outside this institution. She's wearing plain clothes, eating a salad, laughing that too-big laugh.

As I'm trying to grasp at this fragment of memory, she moves over to my bed, smiling.

"Good morning, Nadia. How are you feeling today?"

I'm frustrated and have to let it go; otherwise, she'll know that I'm not drugged. It takes everything in me to release the fragment of my old life and paste on my lopsided smile.

"Good morning, Nurse Delaney. I'm fine, thanks."

She chats about the weather outside as she hands me my paper cup, and I pretend to throw back my pill. I open my mouth to show her it's gone, and she moves on, satisfied.

As she leaves, I desperately try to pull the memory back, but it's gone. The pushing sensation has fled, and I'm left with an image of her smiling in the sunshine, eating a salad, but nothing more.

I punch my pillow, upset that I had to let it get away to continue skipping pills.

Mary looks over. "Everything okay, Nadia?"

"No," I tell her honestly. "Being sober and trying to recover my memories while staying off my pills and not getting caught feels like fighting for my life. I had a flash of a memory, but I had to let it go to pretend that I'm a 'good girl' taking my pills. I'm trying so hard to recover what I can, and this feels like a setback."

"At least memories are trying to surface. I know it's frustrating, but overall, isn't it a good thing?" She cocks her head slightly to the side and sounds sympathetic.

I sigh. She's right. "Yes. Overall, it is a good thing. But it's so irritating to be on the verge of remembering and have it pulled away from you."

"I'm sure. I'm thankful to have my memories. I hope you get them back."

"Thanks, Mary." I get up and walk towards the door, and she follows me. Then I realize Judy 1 is still sitting in her bed.

"Time to go, Judy." I touch her on the shoulder to signal that I'm speaking to her.

She looks up. "Oh, thank you." She starts to get out of bed. "Time for what?"

"Breakfast, Judy. Time for breakfast."

"Oh, okay. Thanks."

We walk out into the hallway in single file toward the dining hall. As I'm shuffling along, I feel Judy 1 step up next to me. I look over.

Judy 1 continues staring straight ahead but asks quietly, "What happened to our other roommate?"

I startle. "What?" Is she asking about Judy 2?

"What happened to her? The other Judy?" Tears spring to her eyes, but they don't fall.

What do I tell her? She seems so fragile since her surgery. I wasn't even sure there was any of the old Judy left inside, but if there is, I don't want to break her.

I decide I have to tell her the truth, as watered down as possible. "She was agitated yesterday, and the nurses took her. Probably just to seclusion." I don't know this for sure, but I really hope it's all that happened.

Judy 1 turns and looks at me. "Is she coming back?"

I have to be honest. "I don't know, Judy. I wish I did."

"Oh, okay. Thanks." Sounding like a small child with her heart breaking, she slows and slips back behind me.

We continue on to breakfast in a single-file line.

Twenty-Two

During breakfast, I try not to stare at Nurse Delaney. I know that the small fragment of memory is from before Ravensbrook. I know her from outside of here.

How? Was she always a nurse? Were we acquaintances before I came here? It's possible, but if that's the case, shouldn't she be trying to help me?

I'm staring into my breakfast mush, trying to puzzle it out, when Mary speaks.

"You're lost again."

I look up. "What?"

"You're lost in your own thoughts. Want to talk about it? It could help." She puts her fork down and rests her chin on a fist.

"I… I don't know how it would help. I'm still just trying to think through the memory from this morning." Especially now, I don't know who I can trust.

"Tell me about it. What was the memory of?" She leans in, interested.

I can't tell her about Delaney. It's too risky. "Just a memory of my Mom, from when I was a kid."

She tilts her head, studying me. "What about it has you frustrated?"

"Oh, just… that it's not complete. That's all." I pick up my fork and start eating, hoping she'll stop playing twenty questions.

She looks like she's going to ask another question and then thinks better of it. She picks up her own fork and finishes breakfast.

Just as we're finishing up, I feel a tap on my shoulder. I try not to, but I startle. Looking up, Delaney is standing next to me.

"Moren, can I see you in my office?" Her smile is cheery, but it feels forced now.

"Y-yes, Nurse Delaney." I paste on my lopsided smile and shoot Mary a quick look. The expression on her face is of worry and a trace of fear.

I need to figure out a way out of this.

Nurse Delaney brings me into a nurse's office and asks me to wait until she's back from morning rounds.

My heart is hammering, and I've started sweating.

Have I been found out?

What is she going to do to me?

Does this have anything to do with the memory?

About fifteen minutes later, Nurse Delaney reenters the office. "Sorry to keep you waiting, Nadia." She sighs and kicks off her shoes.

Something is strange, and it takes me a minute to realize what's different. She's talking to me like I'm human right now.

She sits behind her desk and folds her hands in front of her. Smiling, she says, "So! The other nurses and I have been talking, and we'd like to present you with an opportunity." Her voice is upbeat but has a false ring to it.

I'm dumbfounded. Why am I here? What opportunity could she possibly have for me? I know I'm supposed to be foggy, so I give her my lopsided smile and wait, patient and compliant, to be told what this "opportunity" entails.

When I don't respond, she clears her throat and starts. "You've been doing so well recently. Staying calm, no arguments, keeping with your treatment plan." She smiles again. "Some of the nurses have been talking about your… talent… for drawing portraits. We would like to give you the opportunity to draw portraits for them. With the holiday season coming up, you know." She stops for a moment and looks at me to confirm I understand.

I know it's not really a request. This is a new expectation of me, as a compliant member of this institution.

I'm still waiting to hear the 'opportunity' part. I continue to smile at her and look as dazed as possible.

Her smile falters slightly, and then she regains it as she continues. "So! What this would mean would be that during OT, you'd be able to sit either in here or one of the other offices on this floor, somewhere quiet, and work on portraits. In exchange, you'll be allowed to keep paper and some other supplies in your room. You know, since you've been on your best behavior."

My mouth is hanging open, and I have to actively try to look dopey instead of as shocked as I actually feel. I slowly turn my lips into a grin, with my eyes open too wide. "You're going to let me draw?" I have to sound excited, but also like I don't fully understand what's being asked of me.

"Yes, yes!" Nurse Delaney is smiling now, glad that I finally understood her good news. "We'll provide you with the supplies and with photos of the people you'll be drawing. There are plenty of nurses and orderlies who are very excited to have you helping out, so this should last straight through the holidays. You can start today, right now, if you're ready."

Part of me is happy that I'll get to sit alone and draw without distractions or having to put on my act, but another piece of me knows that this is only being allowed because it serves them. It's a perk that sounds like an opportunity on the surface, but lurking below is just another way they can use me to their advantage.

"Thank you, Nurse Delaney! I'm just happy to draw." My voice is slightly too high and sounds hollow, but she doesn't seem to notice.

She opens the desk drawer and pulls out standard-size paper, some Prismacolor pencils, and graphite pencils. "This is what we have for now. If this occupational endeavor of yours goes well, we can probably chip in and get you some charcoal or a small set of pastels. But we'll see how it goes first." She puts the items on top of the desk, along with five photos. "Are you okay here?" She looks at me, studying my face.

"Yes, thank you, Nurse Delaney."

She nods, satisfied that I'll stay here as expected. Then she departs, leaving me alone in her wake.

I look around the small office. There's a desk with a chair behind it, and two visitors' chairs, one of which I'm currently sitting in. There are posters on the wall. One is a kitten hanging from a bar with "Hang in there, Baby" across the top. Another is a sunset with "HOPE" plastered across it.

They must use this office to meet with family who are leaving their loved ones here. It's still a depressing place, but much cheerier than other spots in the institution.

There's a small table along the side of the wall, so I take the supplies and spread out to give me space to work.

I look at each photo. There's a man, three boys, and a girl. I choose the girl first and begin to sketch her on the paper. I take my time for two reasons. I don't want to rush them because I take pride in my work, but also because if I finish them quickly, this work could be over before it begins.

Having a private space to work is nice. It's the first time I've been truly alone with my thoughts in as long as I can remember. I can sketch, think, and continue planning in peace.

After spending thirty minutes on the first portrait, I hold it up to take a look. It's a beautiful likeness of the child in the photo. I used just a small amount of color; I think I prefer black and white. But I don't think that's what the nurses want.

I choose another child from the stack of photos and begin. Another thirty minutes fly by, and just as I'm putting the finishing touches on the second portrait, Nurse Delaney opens the door.

She takes a few steps over to the table. "Oh my, these are beautiful!" She puts a hand to her chest as if the portraits have touched her. "Maryellen and Ruth are going to be so excited about these!"

I don't make eye contact and sit until I'm told to move.

She looks at me, then realizes I'm waiting for instructions. "Nadia, you can take the paper and supplies back to your room before coming to lunch." She hands me a manila folder to store everything in.

"Thank you, Nurse Delaney." I stand and put the items in the folder before making my way to the door. As I'm exiting, I have a thought and turn around. "Nurse Delaney?"

"Yes, Nadia?"

"Could I possibly get a clipboard so I can work in my room during quiet hours?"

"Of course, hon. I'll bring you one after lunch."

I thank her again and go back to my room to put my supplies away in my bureau drawer.

Walking back to the lunchroom, I ruminate on how strange the last week has been. I became lucid again, witnessed horrors nobody should see, and started to regain memories. I know others will come back too, the longer I'm away from my meds.

Now, I'm being allowed to have pencils and paper in my room. It's all very confusing, honestly.

The only thing I want to happen next is to get out of here.

Twenty-Three

Lunch is quiet.

Betty found a new table to sit at, probably because the rest of us don't talk anymore.

I don't blame her. Judy 1 doesn't usually speak unless she's spoken to, and even then, she has nothing of substance to add to a conversation.

These days, I don't say much, even though I don't think I did before either. Most of the time, Mary is still staring at nothing, though occasionally she'll break and speak briefly, quietly.

Today, she is staring straight at me. "So?"

I look up at her. "What?"

"What?" She looks at me, astounded. "The nurse pulled you out of breakfast, and you were gone for all of OT. What happened?" She looks concerned and slightly confused.

"Oh, that." I smile at her. "So, they want me to draw portraits of their kids and husbands. They like my sketches." I can't help but keep smiling as I look down. I'm strangely proud of my newfound hobby, and I'm good at it. I glance back up at her.

She isn't smiling. "You aren't worried that they're using you? Because of your talent?"

My smile drops. "Well, yeah, they are using me. Of course, they are. But at least I get to sit out basket weaving and painting."

Mary smiles tightly. "I guess so. I just hate to think that you're doing something so nice for them when they'd dose you into oblivion in an instant if they realized you haven't been taking them." She whispers it quietly, but realizing what she said out loud, she covers her mouth in surprise.

"Shh! Are you seriously going to say that right in the middle of the dining hall?" I'm fuming now. Is she trying to get me caught? Can I not trust Mary, either?

Judy 1 looks up. "Who is using you?" She hadn't really been listening, but caught that part.

I glare at Mary as I give Judy an answer. "Oh, the nurses just want me to draw pictures of their kids for them. It's not a big deal."

"That's nice," Judy replies, then goes back to her lunch.

I whisper angrily to Mary, "Don't ever talk about what I'm doing in a public place."

"Sorry," she says, looking down. "I didn't mean to. I just hate to see them taking advantage."

I get up to bring my tray over to the trash cans. As I'm shuffling away, I hear a loud clanging noise.

Suddenly, I'm pressed to the floor: belly down, cheek on the linoleum. Hands splayed by my face. My ears are ringing, and the smell of the dining hall is nauseating. I don't even remember getting to the floor; it just happened.

I get to my knees and use a nearby table to stand up. Looking around, everyone's attention was directed to the metal tray that had fallen over. Nobody saw my descent. That's for the best.

Why on earth did I hit the floor when I heard that noise? It seems as if my body is remembering things that my mind isn't yet capable of.

I sketch the other three portraits during quiet time, while mulling over everything that happened at lunch.

Mary doesn't try to speak or even look at me. She remains on her bed, staring.

The little girl sits on the bed next to me, drawing with her own set of colored pencils.

I look over. She's doing a great job for a kid.

She looks up and smiles. "You're doing a great job too."

I can't help but smile back. "Thanks. Is drawing somehow related to my past?"

She thinks for a moment, tapping her chin with the blunt end of the pencil. "I think so. I don't think you're an artist, though. At least not mostly."

I don't know what that means. I wish this child knew more than I do.

I agree with her. I can sketch, but I can't paint or sculpt, at least from what I've seen during OT.

"Yeah, it's pretty clear I'm not so much an 'artist' as someone who can draw." I turn back to the sketch in front of me of one of the boys. "I'm good at portraits, though." I set aside the last one and pick up a new sheet of paper. My pencil runs over the paper, shaping a cheek, an eye, a hairline. I realize I'm sketching Vic.

The little girl looks over. "He's handsome. He looks like Prince Charming."

I laugh. "I guess he sort of does. But I think he's more rugged than Prince Charming." I continue sketching his mouth, his eyebrows, and his chin.

I pause for a second. Something feels off. I'm not sure what it is. It almost feels like the hint of a memory, flirting with surfacing. It doesn't, and then it's gone. My chest clenches for half a second, then releases. I finish sketching Vic and start another portrait of Mom.

The little girl is watching intently as my mother's face takes shape. "Who is that?"

"My mom. She and my dad came to visit a few days ago." I sketch her cheekbone, then start working on the softness of her hair.

"You look like her."

This revelation stuns me. I stop drawing and look down at the portrait, then over to the little girl.

"Do I?" I don't remember what I look like. There aren't mirrors here. No need to make sure your mascara isn't running or that you don't look as if you stayed up all night.

All of us look washed out, dull, gray. We are collectively the same, so looking into any face here is like looking into a mirror.

"You do," the girl says softly. "You have her eyes and her high cheekbones. Her hair is lighter, but she bleaches it." She thinks for a moment, then continues. "She has always cared about 'looking nice' in a way that isn't important to you."

I've moved past stunned to shocked. "You remember?" My mind is racing now. I know this little girl is part of my own psyche. Does she hold secrets that I can't uncover on my own?

She looks at me, a slight hint of sadness in her eyes. "I remember some things. Not everything. I can only help if you know what you need to know. Even that has limits. You know that."

I do know that. She only knows what I already know but haven't uncovered yet.

I close my eyes and picture my mom. The memory comes, clear as if I had never forgotten in the first place. She was always standing in front of her vanity mirror, fussing with her hair or applying just a touch of blush. Checking her lips in a compact mirror to see if she needed more lipstick. Fussing with my hair, which was always wild and unkempt.

I can't believe the little girl just uncovered this for me, as if I'd never lost it. I look over at her. "Thank you."

She smiles, looking slightly shy. "You're welcome."

Nurse Delaney is delighted that I finished the other portraits during quiet time and tells me that she'll have more photos for me after dinner.

I spend activity time sketching for myself. Letting my brain draw faces that I don't recognize, but I must know.

A woman, who could be a younger version of Mom, appears on the page. After what the little girl said, I may be drawing my own face.

A man, handsome in a studious way. I have no idea who he is.

Another woman and a man, children, even a dog, show up on the pages in front of me. I don't know who any of them are, but my brain does. Somewhere in there are memories of these people. I hope that eventually I can name all of them and figure out their places in my life.

One thing I'm certain of is that I wasn't alone before coming here. I had people I loved and who loved me.

Vic appears on another page, again. Why him? I know we were close as kids, are we close as adults? Do I like his girlfriend? I can feel the slight throb of a memory beginning to push at my brain, but as I try to grasp it, we are called for dinner.

I look at the little girl and whisper, "Can you help me later? To remember?"

She smiles at me. "I'll try as hard as I can."

Dinner passes, and as promised, Nurse Delaney gives me another handful of photos to work from. She again expresses how pleased she is with how quickly I'm working and the quality of the portraits I'm creating. She tells me the staff decided to buy better-quality paper this week, so I'll have real art paper to work on.

Mary doesn't speak, but she makes eye contact. I know exactly what she's thinking. The better-quality paper is for the nurses, not for me.

"Thank you, Nurse Delaney." As much as I know Mary is right, I'm still glad to have something to work on that I enjoy. And it's so much easier to have paper to write my notes on. I don't have to hide them in my pillow anymore.

During evening break, I sketch one more portrait for the nurses. When it's finished, I work on my own. I draw the little girl again, this time coloring her dress emerald green and adding a rosy glow to her cheeks.

I look over at her. Her face doesn't quite match what I've sketched. She looks tired, worn out. She doesn't seem to shine as much as she did before. The bounciness that I used to find slightly irritating is nearly gone. Pajamas have replaced her green dress. Has this place gotten to her, too?

I almost ask if she's okay, then remember that we're not somewhere where we can talk safely.

A short time later, we're back in 108 for rounds and lights out.

Delaney is here distributing meds, so I know that the door will be locked tonight.

I give her the sketch I did after dinner, and she thanks me for creating portraits for everyone.

She leaves, and I grab my materials to continue sketching until lights out.

I look over at Mary, but she's already lying down. She hasn't spoken to me since lunch. I'm not sure if I hurt her feelings or if she's just decided that I'm not worth risking her own neck for.

The little girl is lying down on the bed as I get up to start my new exercise routine. She sees me looking and turns her head. "I'm supposed to help you, right?"

I start. It had completely slipped my mind, the memory that has something to do with Vic. "Thanks for the reminder. I completely forgot."

She smiles. "That's kind of what I'm here for."

"Okay, so what do you know?" I'm eager to hear what my brain is actively hiding from me.

She screws up her face, thinking. "I'm not exactly sure. Are you certain the memory was Vic?"

"I know that it started to come forward while I was looking at the portrait of Vic. Should I get it out of my folder?" Without waiting for her answer, I go to the drawer, pull the portrait out, and study it.

Nothing.

I look at the little girl. "What am I missing?"

"This isn't the same as before. You were relaxed and happy. Now you're trying too hard." She turns back and faces the ceiling. "You have to let the memory come. You can't force it."

I walk back to the bed and lie down, holding the portrait of Vic. I stare at it a moment, then close my eyes. I picture our last visit, him sitting across from me with his arms folded across his chest.

I feel a flutter in the recesses of my mind. Worrying it will go out like a rushed campfire, I sit with the flutter for a moment. Opening my eyes to look again at the portrait, I don't stare. I gaze at it softly as if I'm admiring someone else's artwork.

The flutter becomes a slow pulse, and I can feel it trying desperately to surface. Still, I let it come on its own. If I try to force it, I'll lose it entirely.

Closing my eyes again, I see a flash of hands. They're not idle; they're softly caressing my arms. My back. There are lips on mine, hot breath on my neck. A softness that belies more than makes sense. I try my best not to strain to remember more, but it's difficult. This memory isn't a flood, it's a trickle. It ebbs away almost before it began.

I look at the little girl. "This doesn't make any sense. Could this be of someone else, and my mind is playing tricks? If this memory has to do with Vic, then either my family is really fucked up, or he isn't my brother."

The thought sends ice shards down my spine.

Oh my god. Is Vic lying to me?

But he's trying to get me released.

Wait, is he?

I'm spiraling now, trying to think through the conversations we've had. My heart beats fast, and I can feel the sweat on my skin. There's a rancid smell to this room that wasn't here a few minutes ago.

There's a click, and then the lights go out.

Great, now I'm stuck with my own thoughts in the dark.

I replay the memory, or the shards of it.

Hands. Lips. Breath.

It can't be Vic, unless we aren't actually related. But if we aren't related, then the one thing I thought I knew about him isn't true. And if that's not true, what else isn't?

Late into the night, I lie in bed, replaying the memory fragment. Trying to make it make sense in the context of what I think I know.

I'm fairly confident that my parents are my parents. The memory of Mom from my childhood is a solid clue that what I've been told in that vein is real.

But now, Vic? I didn't see his face in this memory. It clashes not only with what I know about him, but also with how I feel about him. Up to this point, I've had the feeling I could really trust him. This throws a giant wrench into it.

Are my memories jumbled? Or is my gut feeling wrong? Both thoughts are extremely unsettling.

I'm going to have to test him the next time he visits. How, I'm not sure just yet.

I don't have many chips in my corner, but I need to know whether he's betraying me.

Twenty-Four

I sleep just a little before it's time to get up for the day. My brain was awake nearly all night, turning over my thoughts like I was polishing rocks.

I don't have any more answers today than I did when I regained the memory yesterday.

Here's what I know: Vic says he's my brother. My gut tells me I can trust him. Sure, he's attractive, but I'm not drawn to him in that way.

Everything about this newly uncovered memory says the opposite: I'm holding two conflicting ideas of what is real.

Only one thing can be true: either my mind is lying to me, or Vic is.

I look over at the little girl. My mind is not 'right.' So, is it possible that this memory isn't real?

I shuffle off to breakfast and sit at my usual table with Judy 1 and Mary. I pass Betty on the way and give her a small smile and a little wave. I want her to know I don't hold a grudge for her finding more interesting company.

She smiles back. I'm glad.

Mary speaks to me. "How are your portraits going?"

I'm surprised. I was sure she was still upset with me. "They're going well. It's nice to have something to do, something that helps me think."

She smiles. "I'm glad it's making you happy." Her smile falters for a moment.

"What?" I ask her.

"Nothing. I don't want to bring it up in public. We can talk later."

At least she took what I said yesterday to heart.

During OT, I sit in the nurse's office, making portraits. It's the most soothing part of my day. Being alone with my thoughts and some pencils is healing in a way I hadn't expected.

Delaney also brought me the craft paper she promised, so this set of portraits looks even better than the last.

I happily sketch away until Delaney comes back to let me know time is up. Handing her the portraits I've completed, I start toward the door.

Suddenly, a thought occurs to me, and I turn around. "Nurse Delaney, when is Judy 2, I mean, Judy, coming back?" I know it's something I'm not supposed to ask, but Nurse Delaney is the only one in the ward I would dare to even try with.

A look crosses her face briefly. Is it fear?

No, that doesn't make sense.

She regains her composure before I can even be sure she lost it. "Dear, she isn't coming back. She's been moved to a different ward altogether. Somewhere with… stricter supervision where her outbursts can be better handled." She crosses the room and touches my arm. With practiced sympathy, she says, "I'm sorry, I know she was your friend."

Something doesn't sit right. They wouldn't move her to a different room, but now she's in a completely different ward?

Smiling my lopsided smile, I say, "Oh, thanks, Nurse Delaney," then turn and make my exit. Shuffling off to lunch, I turn this information over.

Judy 2 was unstable and explosive. It makes sense they would move her to a place with more supervision, but the timing feels off. Like, there's a piece missing from this puzzle.

I sit down at the table with my tray. There must be a look on my face, because Mary and Judy 1 look over at me.

"What's going on?" they say, almost in unison.

Do I tell them? I guess it can't hurt. At least it gives Judy 1 some closure.

"I asked Nurse Delaney when Judy is coming back. She said she's been moved to a ward with higher supervision, and she isn't coming back." I look up to see Judy 1's reaction.

There's a look of shock on her face, and a sob catches in her throat. "She isn't coming back?"

I'm surprised. I had no idea there was still any part of the Judy 1 I knew left inside her. "I'm so sorry, Judy."

Her hands shake, and her eyes fill up. "I miss her. I'm sad." She sounds like a child being told that a parent had to leave to get milk.

I reach across the table and take her hand, squeezing it. "I know. I miss her, too."

We sit a moment, hands clasped.

Judy 1 lets go and picks up her fork. "She's never, ever coming back?"

My heart breaks for this poor woman. She's lost the very essence of herself, and now she's lost someone she loved, and who loved her in return. "I don't know, Judy. Anything could happen."

She looks up innocently. "So, maybe?"

Everything in me wants to protect the small part of Judy 1 still inside this shell. "Maybe, Judy. You never know."

A small smile crosses her face. She's satisfied now that it might not be forever.

I briefly wish I were pacified that easily.

I spend most of the rest of the day sketching. I use the craft paper only for the nurse's portraits. They'd be upset if I used the paper they bought with their personal money for my own sketches.

While I'm sitting at the end of my bed waiting for nightly rounds, Nurse Trevany pops in to administer them.

She comes over to my bed first to see what I'm sketching.

I'm sketching the house on Pebble Drive, letting my fingers create the memory that I can't picture myself.

She picks the clipboard up for a better look. "This is beautiful, Nadia." Handing it back to me, she adds, "You sketched my little girl yesterday, and did such a beautiful job." There's a tear in her eye, and she places her hand on her heart. "You truly have an amazing talent. Don't ever stop drawing."

"Thank you, Nurse Trevany."

She administers meds to everyone, then leaves the door unlocked.

I look over, and the little girl is staring at me. "Is it time?"

"Time for what?" I ask her. I know what she means, but I'm afraid.

Maybe I can convince her I don't know what she's talking about. These last few days have been significantly better than the previous few months. Could I live with the treatment I'm getting now? It's definitely more bearable than it was. Most of the nurses and a good number of the orderlies are nice to me since I started drawing for them.

She tilts her head. "Really?"

I sigh. I know I can't hide anything from her, any more than I can hide my thoughts and feelings from myself.

"Do I have to?"

"Don't you want to?" She looks at me sadly, like I'm disappointing her.

"Yes. No. I don't know anymore." The few comforts I've received have been enough to make me question whether I'm doing the right thing.

She looks past me to Judy 1. "You have to do it for her." She looks over to Mary, "And her, as much as for yourself. For Judy 2, too."

I put my head in my hands. I hate that she's right.

Twenty-Five

I try to sleep, knowing that it will be hours before I can realistically sneak out. I'm restless, and what little sleep I get is fraught with nightmares.

I wake, and I know it's late by the darkness outside, mirrored by the dark hallway. There's an ominous feeling in the air, and the smell of antiseptic is strong. Standing up, I look at the little girl.

She nods at me, urging me to find my courage.

I know she's right, but I'm scared. Now I have something to lose, however small it is.

As I walk by Judy 1, I stop to check on her.

She looks so small and pure, lying there asleep.

My heart lurches, and it steadies my resolve.

The little girl is right. I have to do this. Nothing in this place is guaranteed, especially my newfound status.

I look over toward Mary, and she's sitting up. "Thank you," she says quietly.

I nod. "It's the right thing to do. For all of us."

Slipping out into the hallway, I'm on high alert for nurse and orderly activity, but the hall is quiet. I begin to walk toward the nurses' station, as silently as possible.

Then, I hear them—the screams.

Stopping short, I listen for a moment. It takes every ounce of determination inside me not to turn around and run back to 108.

Truly, this is a good thing. Not for the woman in the procedure room, of course. But it means that the staff aren't in the nurses' station; they're all crowded around their patient.

Torturing her.

I shudder, thinking about what happens in that room. Moving down the hall, I slow as I come to the station. As expected, it's empty. I don't bother to move past it to see the horrors going on just down the hall.

The door to the records room stands ajar. I slip inside and stop, looking at the different drawers. Where do I even start?

I move over to the drawer labeled "Research Studies." What is Judy 2's last name? Thinking a moment, it comes to me. Dean. Her last name is Dean. I open the drawer and move through the files until I get to D. I continue flipping until I see it:

Dean, Judith.

I take a breath and open the file. Scanning the document, I see she has been here for about eighteen months. She's been on Thorazine, Lithium, and Haldol. She's undergone ECT twice. Seclusion a dozen times at least. Pretty normal for this place. Nothing screams 'illegal' to me.

I keep scanning, then come to the last item on the chart.

Neuro Mapping indicated.

It's dated two days ago.

What the hell is neuro mapping? My heart beats slightly faster, and I can feel and taste the bile rising in my throat.

Is what happened to my friend the evidence I need?

I look down again at her chart, and my heart stops.

Neuro-mapping discontinued due to loss of neurological response.

That can't mean what it sounds like.

Preservation team notified. Transfer initiated.

What the fuck is a preservation team? My mind is spinning, and I stagger backward, gripping a small table that sits just inside the doorway.

Even reeling, I know I need to uncover what this means with more certainty.

I close the Research Studies drawer and practically rip open "Patient Outcomes." As quickly as I can, I flip through the D's until I find it. *Dean.*

There are fewer of these files, and they list only the last name. Opening the folder, it's a much smaller chart than the last one. There's just a list of her procedures. I scan it as quickly as possible, because I know I'm running out of time. I need to get back to my room before they wheel their current patient into the hall, and the screams stopped what feels like ages ago.

Patient Outcomes: Dean, Judith
Subject transferred to Research Unit
Neuro-mapping initiated
Adverse neurological event noted
Nonresponsive to intervention
Neuro-mapping discontinued
Primary physician notified
Support withdrawn per protocol
Preservation prep authorized
Time of death: 3:47 am
Transfer to Mortuary completed
Family Notified
Patient File closed

This can't be real. I sit hard on the ground, trying to process what I just read.

They killed her.

They killed Judy.

I don't understand a lot of the words in the file. But I know what "time of death" and "mortuary" mean. She's been murdered.

My breath comes in spasms. My eyeballs feel hot and dry when I should be in tears. Panic is taking over. I know I need to take the file, so I fight through it.

Standing up, I go back to the drawer. Opening it, I accidentally overshoot the "D" section and right past the whole alphabet. Towards the back of the drawer is another folder labeled "Grant Money — Seeds."

What on earth? I open this file and stop in my tracks. It's a list of all the experimental surgeries that have been performed, paid for directly by Horizon Biomedical Group to Ravensbrook. There's a list pages long of different surgeries that have been performed here: amygdalotomy, neuro-mapping, deep-brain electrode implants, cingulotomy, and … oh God … *organ harvesting.*

There it is, in black and white. Dollar signs on paper, as if the lives they took were nothing more than a product for sale.

I can't accept what I'm reading. It has to be my psychosis acting up at just the wrong time. Right? How long have I been standing here? I have no idea what time it is. I need to get back to my room.

As I'm closing the drawer, I spot a folder that catches my eye: Moran.

I want to look at my chart, see how many times I've had ECT, if they've done anything else to me that may be illegal, but I don't have time. I'm going to have to come back another night; staying right now is too risky.

I exit the room and see that the station is still empty. In the hallway, I begin to creep back to safety when I hear the doors to the procedure room start to swing open, the squeaking of the gurney unmistakable.

Breaking into a run, I book it down the hall until I get to my room. Thinking fast, I lock the door behind me as I rush in, and it clicks shut. I jump into bed and pull the covers up, breathing hard. A moment later, two orderlies rush past the room, looking for whoever was in the building. I can hear them shouting to each other.

I lie in bed, trying to catch my breath and process everything I just learned.

Judy 2 is dead.

They murdered her by experimenting on her.

They have a file for me.

Am I next?

Tears pour silently out of me and onto my pillow.

Judy 2 didn't deserve this. It's a violation of everything they say they're doing here. Here I was worried about Judy 1 and them taking her essence away, and they took Judy 2's life.

I sit up.

Delaney lied right to my face this morning. What was it she said? *A different ward with stricter supervision for her outbursts.*

She's a liar. Judy 2 is dead, and there's no way she doesn't know it.

As I continue processing, I hear the orderlies walking back toward the nurses' station.

"Could we have hallucinated it? It is really late."

The voice sounds younger, slightly upset.

The other sounds old and gruff. "No, we didn't hallucinate it, you dolt. We heard someone running down the hall. They must have snuck in and gotten back out before we could catch up to them."

If nothing else, at least I managed to get back without getting caught. Their suspicions have turned toward an outsider and not a patient.

I lie down and stare into the darkness. Then a thought occurs to me, and I bolt upright again, sweating.

Judy 2's neuro-mapping was two nights ago.

The last time I snuck out.

I witnessed her last moments.

The taste of bile is back in my throat, and I feel nauseous. The room spins as I try to steady myself. I can feel the sweat dripping down my back.

My vision blurs. The last thing on my mind before I pass out from disgust and fear is the sound of the drill, followed by Judy 2's screams.

Twenty-Six

I wake the next morning feeling weak and sick. When the nurse comes in for morning rounds, I'm unable to lift my head off the pillow.

She puts her hand to my forehead. "Nadia, you're burning up. Let's get you to the sick ward. Can you walk?"

I try to stand, but my legs won't hold me.

She leaves and comes back with a wheelchair.

I'm wheeled down the hall to the sick ward. I don't know if I've ever been here before, but it doesn't look familiar.

The nurse helps me out of the chair and into a bed. She shakes a thermometer and sticks it under my tongue. Next, she checks my blood pressure, then listens to my lungs with the stethoscope. "Deep breaths, hon." With a penlight, she looks into my eyes, checking my pupils.

"Yep. You're sick." She gives me a dose of acetaminophen. "Hopefully, this will take the fever down, and you'll feel a little better."

I lie in bed and drift in and out of consciousness. Each time I wake, I think about Judy 2. About what they did to her, and how much of it I witnessed. When I fall asleep, I hear her screams and the squeaking of the gurney. I smell burnt flesh and antiseptic.

There is no break; it's on my mind either way.

At some point, I wake and hear Nurse Delaney's voice.

"What's wrong with her?"

"Probably just a little bug, maybe a touch of the flu. She should be better in a couple of days, nothing to worry about."

Most of the day, I drift in and out. Sometimes I wake and hear the nurse humming to herself or talking to another patient. Other times, it's the metal-on-metal noise of a curtain being pulled back or the creaking of a cart being pushed around. Once it was so quiet I could hear the clock on the wall, ticking the day away.

The nurse wakes me up to administer more meds and tells me that my dinner is here. Did I eat breakfast or lunch? I don't think I did.

She senses my confusion. "I didn't wake you for the other two meals, but I figured you haven't eaten today, you should probably try."

I take a real look at her for the first time today. She's young, probably right out of training. She seems genuinely nice. I'm guessing she hasn't been here long, and the world of institutional life hasn't come crashing down on her yet. Or maybe the sick ward is its own little pocket of calm, and it's a different reality here.

"Thank you," I tell her, sitting up in bed.

She smiles. "You're welcome, hon. Try to eat slowly. You need the energy, but your fever hasn't broken yet." Then she walks away to check on another patient.

I look down at my tray. There's a small paper cup with my pill in it. At least I don't have to lie to this lovely young nurse. When she's turned completely away from me, I take the pill and stick it in my sock.

Looking down at the tray, I pick at the parts that look edible. I'm really not that hungry. I'm not sure what I am right now. Sick, sad, angry, and disgusted, for starters.

There's one thing I know: I need to take the evidence and get it out. I need this place shut down for the sake of everyone here. I wish I'd had more time for the shock to wear off last night; the files could already be stashed in my room, waiting for Vic to visit.

Vic. God, I'd almost forgotten that I don't know if I can trust him.

I put my head in my hands. Who *can* I trust? He may be my only hope.

The young nurse comes by. "You okay, hon? You didn't eat much."

"I'm okay, just not very hungry. Still a little nauseous." I don't know if I'll ever be able to eat again.

She looks at the tray before taking it back to a waiting food cart. "Well, at least you got your meds down. Good girl." She smiles at me as she walks away.

I'm far from the 'good girl' they all seem to think I am lately. But let them believe it; it keeps me off anyone's radar.

By the next morning, my fever has broken. The young nurse is here again, and I ask her how long I can stay.

She laughs. "You like my sick ward, huh? It's no hotel."

"Neither is the rest of the place," I tell her with a smile.

She smiles back. "I'll probably keep you at least until lunch, see if you can hold a couple of meals down. I don't want you back here tonight. No offense."

"None taken. I'd rather feel well, too." It's a half-truth. This is by far the best place in the building. She's attentive, kind, and mostly hands-off unless you really need something. She makes you feel human in a way that the rest of the staff doesn't.

Now that I feel physically better, I treasure every moment I get to stay in the sick ward. It feels safe here, and I can truly relax.

I think about Judy 2. About the files. About *my* file. I wonder if I can't get out of here, if my fate will be like either of the Judys. I question how long it will take to get the name misspelling fixed, and if that's even a real issue.

A few times, I tear up, but I don't cry. It's hard, not knowing if my own memory is trustworthy. The confusing memory of Vic is the one thing that leads me to believe he can't be trusted.

The day wears on, and by lunchtime, I know I'm going to be dismissed back to my ward. I'm feeling much better, and they'll need the bed for the next person with the flu.

After lunch, the nurse walks me back to 108 for quiet time. Nurse Delaney is waiting for me in the room.

"How are you feeling, hon? I came by the sick ward yesterday to check on you, but you were sleeping." She looks slightly haggard today.

I throw on my signature smile. "Oh, thanks for asking. I'm feeling much better today. Must have been a twenty-four-hour bug." Sitting on my bed, I wait for her to hand me new photos. I know that's why she's really here.

She smiles. "Good, glad to hear it. Oh, I brought some new photos today, too. I know you still have a couple from the day before yesterday, but you've been getting through them so quickly that I thought it would help." Then, realizing how callous that sounded, she adds, "But don't feel like you have to get to them today. I know you're still recovering."

"Thank you, Nurse Delaney. I'll try." I lay down on the bed to signal that I'm done chatting.

She seems taken aback. "Oh, right. Okay, you rest up, and I'll check in with you later." She closes the door softly behind her.

"Well, that was rude." Mary is sitting up and looking at me. "You just got back from the sick ward, and she's in here hounding you for free portraits."

"It's okay, Mary. If I get to them, I do. If I don't, then they'll live." I turn over, away from her. I know she's mad at the staff because she doesn't like watching them use me, but right now that is the least of my worries.

I sleep some, but it's still fitful. Brief nightmares about being in the procedure room. The smell of blood and burnt hair. Judy 2 as the surgeon. When I wake, the nightmare fades, but reality is nearly as harsh.

An orderly opens the door. "Activities! Moren, Visitor!"

Terrific. Just what I need when I'm trying to physically recover from illness and emotionally sort out everything I learned yesterday. I don't know if I can tolerate a visit from Vic.

Yet, I still need him. At a minimum, I need this visit to determine whether or not I can trust that he's on my side.

Sighing, I get out of bed. Judy 1 has already left. Mary follows me out the door. I notice she looks tired, like she hasn't been sleeping well.

"You okay?" I ask her.

She smiles weakly. "I'm okay. Just feeling a little run-down. Hopefully it passes quickly."

We split off as she heads to the activity room, and I open the door to the visitors' lounge.

Twenty-Seven

Vic is sitting in the same corner as during his last visit. I guess this is our spot now, as far away from our chaperones as possible. He looks tired, but when he sees me, his eyes light up briefly. Then concern crosses his face, and lines appear between his eyebrows.

"Are you okay?" he asks as I sit down. "You look terrible."

"Gee, thanks. Nice to see you too." I can't help but smile, even as a wave of nausea comes over me. His concern feels genuine, even if he isn't the best at putting it into words.

He rubs the back of his neck. "Sorry, that was probably harsh, huh?"

"Yeah, but it's okay. I've been sick for the last couple of days. I just got back to my room from the sick ward."

"I'm glad you're feeling better. I wish I had better news to bring you, but I'm still fighting through the red tape. For a minute, I felt like I was getting somewhere, but now it's hung up again, waiting on a judge." He runs his fingers through his hair, and there is a look of sadness in his eyes. He pauses, then adds, "Have you remembered anything else? Besides the memory of Mom?"

I'm supposed to be interrogating him, and here he is, interviewing me instead. How do I test him? Something occurs to me, and I decide to roll with it.

"Not so much a memory, but I've discovered I can draw. I'm great at portraits. Is that something I've always had a talent for?" I need to see if he squirms at this, or if the answer comes naturally.

"Oh, right." He thinks for a moment. "You always were pretty good. You took a class, maybe ten years ago, that brought you from good to really great. So, I guess the real answer is yes, you were always talented. Even from grade school." There's no hint of him sweating or his face twitching in a way that makes me think he's lying. He gives a short laugh. "I'm pretty sure you filled the margins of every notebook with doodles. They ended up being more drawings than notes."

I decide I don't have much choice but to trust him. He's the only path forward.

"Things have gotten terrible here," I whisper.

His eyes go wide. "Have they done something to you?"

"Probably, but that's not what this is about. They have a filing cabinet full of paperwork." I look behind me to see that nobody is listening. "There's a list of all the experimental treatments that have been performed here. There's even a file showing how much money the institute was paid for each surgery."

Vic practically leaps out of his chair and is now standing. "Are you serious?"

The nurse looks over. "Everything okay over there?"

I think fast, speaking loudly. "Vic, sit down. Mom and Dad didn't upset me when they came to visit. They were very calm."

Vic, realizing his mistake, looks over at the nurse. "Sorry for the outburst. I was worried they might complicate her treatment." He sits.

The nurse nods. "Let's try to keep the voices down, okay? We don't need to upset her or the other patients." She goes back to reading a book.

"You almost blew that one. Staying calm is the number one way I've managed to keep my wits about me.

Well, mostly, at least." I look over to the little girl, playing jacks on the floor. She's my constant reminder that my mind is not entirely right.

"Sorry, I just… I can't believe that you found all that. How did you do it?" He reaches over and takes my hand, squeezing it.

"I just knew I had to find something. And while it's not like there's a spotlight beaming onto the paperwork, it's not very well hidden. They're really relying on all of us being so doped up that we can't see straight." My eyes well up as I think of the Judys and the harm that's been done.

"What? What is it?" His voice is urgent but caring.

"I found out that one of my friends was…" I look over to the nurse. Her face is buried in her book. Turning back to Vic, I mouth the word, "Murdered."

His eyes fly open in shock. "Are… are you sure? How have they gotten away with this?" I can see his hands are shaking now. He's as terrified as I am.

I sigh. "I'm sure. And I don't know how long this has gone on, but I need to get that paperwork to you. We need to close this place down before anyone else gets hurt. What's going on here is absolutely criminal."

I can't shake the feeling that he's not my brother, but my gut still says I can trust him. With my mind as twisted as it is, I'm going to have to trust my gut.

I spend the rest of the day recovering in my room. I'm still weak and slightly shaky. Whether this is from the bug or from the realization of how dark everything here actually is, I can't be sure.

I'm not feeling up to sketching, so when Delaney comes by before bed, I have nothing to turn over.

She soothingly tells me not to worry about it, that we can always try again tomorrow.

I don't trust her. Anyone, really. But there's something she knows that I don't. That's one of the only things I'm sure of. I will keep her at arm's length and play the role of the dutiful patient for as long as I have to.

Sleep comes easily for a change. Exhaustion from my illness and emotional state is something that isn't in short supply.

In the morning, I wake up rested and feeling slightly better. Shuffling off to breakfast with Mary and Judy 1, I attempt to eat.

Judy 1 is quiet, as always.

Mary asks if I'm feeling okay.

"I'm starting to feel better, thanks. How about you?" She looks less run-down than yesterday.

"I'm okay, too. Thanks." She eats a forkful of eggs, thinking while she chews. "Is everything *else* okay?" She looks at me like she can tell I'm hiding something.

"Um…" I look over at Judy 1, then back to Mary. "Not here. I can't."

Mary nods, understanding that whatever I've uncovered, we can't discuss it in public. "Quiet time, then?"

"Quiet time. Be prepared. It's brutal."

Twenty-Eight

I spent OT in the office, drawing. Delaney brings me even more photos, so I now have a backlog of about a dozen. I'm not going to rush through them. I'll take my time, finding joy in creating each distinct portrait.

I've finished three and started on a fourth before lunchtime.

Lunch is quiet, as meals typically are now. It flies by, and before I know it, we're back in 108 for quiet time.

Judy 1 lies down and closes her eyes.

I turn and see Mary looking at me expectantly, but before I can tell her that I want to make sure Judy 1 is asleep, she blurts out, "You found something about Judy 2. Something horrific."

My eyes go wide, and I look over to Judy 1, whose eyes are still closed.

"Can you wait 'til we know she's asleep?" I hiss at her. "Also, how on earth did you know that?"

Judy 1 opens her eyes. "Who are you talking to?"

Mary and I look at each other sadly. I turn back to her. "Judy, I'm talking to Mary." I gesture in Mary's direction.

Judy 1 sits up and looks over at Mary, confusion on her face.

This poor woman. They've taken every ounce of logic out of her. Now her recognition of people is going too?

"Nadia, who is Mary? There isn't anyone there." The confusion is evident in her voice. She looks skeptical, like I'm playing a trick on her.

I look over at Mary again. She's sitting in bed, plain as the nose on my face. "Judy, she's sitting right on her bed, where she always sits. Mary, our other roommate."

Judy 1's face softens. "Oh, Nadia. I'm so sorry, but we are the only people in this room."

I look over at Mary. She doesn't seem disturbed by Judy's blatant disregard for her.

A chill begins to creep up my spine.

"Mary?" I look at her hard. "Come over here, so Judy can see you clearly."

Mary gets out of bed and walks over, standing right in front of Judy 1.

"See, Judy? She's right there. Right in front of you." I'm sweating now, and my mouth tastes like old cigarettes.

Judy looks at me sympathetically. "Nadia, Mary isn't real. I know you talk to her all the time. Here, meals, sometimes in OT or activity time, but she's not a real person. She's in your head."

Mary looks down at the floor.

"Mary? MARY. Look at me." I'm terrified and furious.

She looks up.

"Are you not real?" I feel feverish again. This can't be happening.

Mary slowly shakes her head. "I'm just another part of you. A part that separated so it didn't break. Just like her," she points to the little girl, who is sitting wide-eyed on the bed next to me.

This is what being insane feels like.

I lie down on my bed. I don't know what is real and what's not anymore.

Mary approaches, but I can't handle this right now. "Mary, I need you to go away. Right now, I can't."

She nods, then turns and goes back to her bed.

I don't know how much more I can take. There is nobody in the world I can trust.

Including myself.

I spend the rest of the day in a haze. Mary tries to speak to me, but I can't acknowledge her just yet. I'm hurt, angry, and scared. It's as if she's been lying to me this whole time. I want to be upset with her, but it's difficult to point fingers at someone who isn't real. Someone who is quite literally me.

I sketch, but the quality isn't as good as it was yesterday or even this morning. My hands shake, and I can't make them stop. I'm stuck in an endless loop of anguish.

Judy 2 and Mary. I feel like they both died.

At dinner, I realize that I don't know if anyone is real. Every person I come in contact with could be an offshoot of my own psyche. Was the nurse in the sick ward real? Are the files I thought I found even real? Didn't that seem slightly too easy?

I spend the rest of the evening unraveling. My mind is coming unglued.

Maybe this is why I'm here, why I asked to come here. I'm not fit for the outside world. No wonder I was a burden to my family. I see people who don't exist and think they are fully human, flesh-and-blood.

After lights out, I look over at the bed next to me. The little girl is sitting cross-legged, waiting. She's usually playing a game or reading a comic, but this time she's biding her time, waiting for me to be ready to talk.

I roll to the other side.

She gets up, walks over to the other bed, and sits down cross-legged.

I sigh. "Honestly, I can't right now. I don't know how to deal with this, so we can't talk about it."

She looks at me warmly, with a hint of sadness. "It's okay. We can think it through together." She looks up, then down at me again. "Maybe Mary can help too."

"No! Neither of you is real, so you can't help. I'm alone in this. Completely, totally, insanely alone." Tears spring to my eyes. I've sunken into a void that I'm not sure I can recover from.

The little girl scoots closer. "It's going to be okay."

I look at her in shock. "How? How is it ever going to be okay? I knew you weren't real. I accepted that my mind created you because it needed to. But her?" I point to Mary, sitting on her bed, looking defeated. "How can I accept this? How will I ever know for sure if someone is real or just another figment of my imagination?"

The tears fall, and I don't try to stop them. I bury my face in the thin pillow and let the weeks, months, probably years, of built-up emotion out. It comes in waves, and my pillow is nearly soaked through by the time I've cried them all out.

I sit up.

Mary is lying down and appears to be asleep.

The little girl is sitting with her back to the wall, next to me, reading a book. She looks up. "It's going to be okay. When you're ready to talk about it, I'm here. So is she." She points over to Mary, but Mary doesn't wake.

I lie down on my wet pillow.

There's no going back from here. No unknowing what I know.

I can only move forward.

Twenty-Nine

I wake the next morning before our scheduled time. Opening my eyes, they're blurry and feel gritty and dry.

Inside, I'm empty. Hollow.

Is this better than being foggy? I'm not so sure anymore.

Mary is sitting up, looking at me.

I shake my head. No. I can't do this. Not yet. I'm still processing everything that has happened over the last few days. I need more time. Acceptance hasn't come yet.

I drift through the day. There's breakfast, then OT. I sketch, and they're better than yesterday because my hands aren't shaking, but something about the drawings feels lifeless. Joyless.

Lunch, then quiet time. I sketch a little bit, but also take a nap. Dreaming feels less empty than my waking life.

An orderly opens the door. "Activity time! Moren, visitor!" He slams it behind him.

Visitor? Wasn't Vic just here the day before yesterday? Could he have news? Right now, I'm so mentally broken that the thought of getting out is more important than saving everyone. I don't even know if they're all real, or if this is a mental hospital of one.

Opening the door to the visitors' lounge, I instinctively look to the corner table for Vic, but it's empty.

I turn to the right and see Dad sitting alone at a table, waiting for me.

This is not what I expected today, and I'm not really prepared to deal with anyone else's emotional needs.

He's looking down, twiddling his thumbs.

"Hi, Dad," I say, sitting across from him.

He starts. "Oh, hi, Nadia." He looks uncomfortable, like he would rather be anywhere else. He isn't here for me, that much is clear.

"How are you?" I ask him.

"I'm fine," he answers gruffly. Looking up, he realizes he needs to ask me the same. "Are you hanging in there?"

"By a thread," I answer honestly. "I've been better."

He looks down again at his hands, and the discomfort is palpable.

This is going to be a short visit, I'm sure of it.

He's avoiding eye contact, and he has no idea how to transition to the reason he's here.

"What's up, Dad? Why the visit? I wasn't expecting anyone." I figure if I have to sit here, at least we can get this show on the road. I'm already angry and bitter. I don't need to add extra emotions to the growing list.

"Well," he says, still playing with his thumbs, "Vic told me that you've been through some things lately. That he's worried." He's not warm; it doesn't feel like this is coming from a place of concern.

"Oh. Yeah, things have been rough." Why is he testing me? "I was in the sick ward for a couple of days with a bug." I instinctively know this isn't the information he's looking for.

"He told me you weren't feeling well." He leans away as if he might catch it. "Anything else going on?"

I think for a moment. "I've been drawing portraits." I'm not toying with him, but I'm unsettled right now. This isn't a warm father/daughter interaction. He's clearly uncomfortable. Has our relationship always been like this?

He flinches. "Right, well, that's good." He leans forward again, shifting in his seat.

I think again of the feeling I had when he and Mom came to visit, like they were mismatched.

"Has anything else happened?" He makes eye contact and puts his hands down on his lap.

Vic told him about Judy 2. "Um… nothing I can think of off the top of my head." Vic obviously trusts him, but something about this interaction is just off.

In my current state, I can't force this trust when I barely trust myself. I'm sure that in real life, outside these walls, I love this man. But sitting in front of me, strange and generic, he's asking too much of me.

"Oh. Your brother thought you had… concerns about something. That something happened." He's the one who looks agitated now.

"Nope, sorry. Guess you came all this way for nothing." I still don't know why he came to visit. It wasn't to support me. Is there a better chance of getting out if I tell him what happened to Judy 2?

"Yeah, well…" He looks up, realizing that he said the wrong thing. "It wasn't for nothing, Nadia. It's good to see you. I'm glad that you're okay." This is the first thing he's said that sounds genuine today.

"Thanks, Dad." I sigh. This man is complicated. But I guess all men his age are, right? I still don't have it in me to tell him anything else right now. My head hurts, and I'm very thirsty. "I appreciate the visit. Maybe you can come by again next week? I'm not feeling so hot right now." I want to go back to bed.

"Right, no problem, honey." He gets up and gives me an awkward hug before turning around to leave. As he reaches the door that leads to freedom, he turns one last time.

"Nadia?" He looks at me softly. It's the gentlest look I've seen on his face.

"Yes?"

"It's going to be okay. We're going to sort all this out and get you out of here. I promise." Then he's gone, the door slamming shut behind him.

The nurse on duty in the visitors' lounge let me return to my room when I told her I was exhausted. Instead of sitting in the activity room, I get to lie down and think.

Judy 1 is at activity time, so I'm alone.

Well, alone as I get these days.

Mary is sitting on her cot, braiding the little girl's shiny blonde hair.

As the door closes behind me, she looks up. "Are you ready to talk yet?"

I throw myself down on the bed, face-first. "I don't know if I'll ever be ready to talk."

"We have to talk about it sometime. You know that."

I look over at the two of them. At the parts of myself that have separated to keep me sane. I bark out a laugh. 'Sane' is probably not the right word for what I am.

Mary looks at me sadly. "It's okay, you know. It's a lot to take in. You weren't ready to hear it, that's why I didn't tell you."

I'm angry. "No, instead, you let me believe you were real. How many conversations did I have with you during meals? During activity time and OT? How many times was I sitting there, literally talking to myself?"

She casts her eyes downward. "I'm sorry. I couldn't tell you, you weren't ready to hear it."

I get up and walk over to Mary's bed and sit down. Reaching for the little girl's hair, I'm expecting to come back with only air. Instead, I pick up a gold strand. My eyes go wide, and I drop it.

"What in the world?" Mary hands me the braid she's working on, and I continue braiding the little girl's hair. "How is this possible? It's not possible. How is it happening?"

Gently, Mary tells me, "Our brains are amazing, and they are very tuned to our sense of touch. It's not real, but it's still happening."

Incredulous, I finish the braid and tie the bottom with an elastic. Leaning forward, I hug the little girl, and she puts her head on my shoulder.

The tears come again. Mary wipes them from my cheeks, and though I can feel her touching me, they still fall.

Thirty

I spend the rest of the day adjusting to my new reality. Mary and the little girl can interact with me, but not with the external world.

They can't open the door or pick up a pencil. They can look over my shoulder as I draw and point out where an eye or a nose needs adjusting, but they can't help erase a mistake.

By the time I'm called for dinner, things have settled a bit. My nervous system has calmed slightly, and I've finished a few portraits, which makes Nurse Delaney happy. As she walks away, Mary sticks her tongue out, and I gasp to keep from laughing. I don't talk with them at dinner. Instead, I try my best to engage Judy 1 in conversation.

"Judy, how are you doing?"

She looks at me, doe-eyed. "I'm fine, thanks, Nadia. How are you?"

We chat superficially. About the weather. The food. I bring up what it would be like to get out of here, and Judy responds, "Oh, that sounds nice."

We don't talk about Mary or Judy 2 or the screams. We don't mention the horrors going on behind so many closed doors here.

It's pleasant, if not meaningful.

After dinner, I join the others in the activity room and sketch. Mary and the little girl sit with me and talk, but they don't expect a reply, and I don't give one.

Later, before lights out, when I'm sure Judy 1 is asleep, we finally speak again.

"Know what I keep thinking about?" I ask.

"Yes," Mary and the little girl reply together. Mary smirks.

"Yeah, I guess you would, wouldn't you? Really, though, remember only a few days ago when I was questioning if all of this is enough? If the portraits and the slight special treatment were worth staying here? When I was contemplating not looking for a way out?"

Mary nods. "I do. But you realized that it's more than that. What's happening here isn't right for anyone."

"I don't think I can try tonight." I hang my head, slightly ashamed.

"It's okay," says the little girl. "Nobody expects you to. A lot has happened, and you need time."

Mary nods again. "She's right. Obviously, going out there is brave, and it's the right thing to do, but not now. Not tonight. You're still trying to process what all of this means for your life. You need to save yourself if you have any chance of saving everyone else."

I know they're right, but there's still some shame in feeling like I can't help tonight. Every night we stay here is another night that could be someone's last.

"Judy 2 would be proud of what you're doing," Mary says quietly. She reaches over and cradles my face. "It's okay to need a moment to think it all through."

The tears come again, as they do frequently these days.

The three of us lay down. I'm on my cot, they're on the beds beside me.

It's comforting.

I'm asleep almost instantly.

For a day or two, I listen to Mary and the little girl. I learn to adjust to the knowledge that they are parts of me, fragments that have split from my brain into separate entities in order to protect them. I question if they're the only parts. The two of them insist they are, but could there be others they aren't aware of?

I think about the file. *Moran.* What have they done to me to cause these parts of my consciousness to split off entirely? Or was I like this before I came here? I intend to find out.

It's just before lights out. I spent the day sketching and talking to Mary and the little girl, working through my thoughts, fears, and hopes. Bouncing scenarios off of them. Thinking about 'what if' we were to get out of here.

Tonight, Nurse Trevany did our nightly rounds. That means it's time.

I take my notes out of my drawer and add to them. If the worst were to happen, I need to know where I stand. I need to remember.

I hear a click, and the lights go out.

I look over, but Judy 1 has been asleep since shortly after Nurse Trevany left.

"You're doing this as much for her as for yourself," Mary says quietly.

She's right. As much as I want to get out of this trauma ward, I want everyone to get out. I know a lot of them will just be placed elsewhere, but maybe those places aren't being funded by experimental tests without the patients' or their families' knowledge. Maybe at least they can sleep at night without fear of their lives being taken away.

Without any warning, I feel it—a memory throbbing in my brain.

I look up. Mary and the little girl feel it too. I don't have to ask. I know.

"Joy," Mary says aloud. She closes her eyes. "Happiness."

I nod. I feel it too. I can almost grasp it. I remember what the little girl said last time. I look at her.

"Yes, you have to relax. Let it be, don't force it." She closes her eyes, too. "I'm wearing a pretty dress, but it's dirty. I'm laughing."

I can see it clearly in my mind's eye as she explains it. "There's a swing. I see a slide. A sandbox. Monkey bars." I open my eyes. "It's a playground!"

The others nod. They see it too.

Mary speaks next. "I can feel the wind in my hair. I'm sliding down. It's exciting!"

"But something's wrong." The little girl frowns.

She's right. Something is wrong. "There's pain," I say. "What happened?" I look at the other two.

The little girl jumps in. "Ow! My knee!"

I see it, plain as day. A scraped knee. I fell off the end of the slide and skinned my knee on a rock. I look at the two of them, ecstatic. "We did it! A full memory!"

"Wait," Mary says. "That's not all."

She's right. I see him. "Someone is coming over to help us up." He's a few years older, with dark hair. Handsome for a ten-year-old kid. He helps me up and over to a half wall to sit down. He leaves, then comes back with a Band-Aid. Carefully wiping the scratch off with his shirt first, he applies the bandage like a surgeon. I smile at him through my tears, and he hugs me. "It's okay, Nadia. It's just a scrape. You'll be fine. Want me to push you on the swing?"

The memory fades out, and I'm left with a beautiful sense of warmth. The boy in that memory cared for me.

"What a beautiful memory," I say aloud.

"I think we had a beautiful childhood," the little girl adds.

If we keep remembering, I may start to agree with her.

Thirty-One

It's the middle of the night. I spent the last few hours replaying the memory, turning it over in my mind. This memory feels like an oasis in the desert. When I close my eyes, I can feel the sun shining on my face, the wind as I slide down, and the pain of the small scrape. I can see the boy tenderly putting the bandage on my knee.

Knowing that I wasn't always this way makes me want to get out and find the rest of my story. I know I'm slowly recovering it here, but I also know that if I were somewhere I could relax, I could regain it so much faster.

I step up to the door, and Mary and the little girl flank me on either side. There's no harm in them coming now. It will make me feel less alone and give me courage. Turning the doorknob, I step into the hall.

The smell of ammonia and disinfectant stings my nose. I have to pinch it so I don't sneeze and alert someone.

The three of us creep down the hall. It's quieter than usual. No sound comes from the nurses' station or the procedure room. The closer we get to the nurses' station, the stronger the smell of coffee becomes.

Mary looks terrified, and the little girl looks like she might cry.

I guess I have to be the brave one.

We tiptoe up to the column by the nurses' station and wait, listening.

Where is everyone? There doesn't seem to be a procedure going on, but the nurses are absent, too.

I slink quietly past the station and over to the procedure room door. Looking inside, it's dark. There's nobody to be found.

Whispering to the others, I tell them, "I think we should go back. Something is off tonight. We can't be out here."

Just as I'm turning back in the direction of 108, I hear footsteps, then a shout.

I take off running, as fast as I can, but it's not fast enough. I'm grabbed and thrown to the floor, with my arms twisted behind my back.

I hear a man yell, "Delaney! We've got an escape artist!"

Oh God, not Delaney. I didn't know she was working tonight. This isn't typically her shift. "No!" I shout as I try to struggle free. "You can't do this!"

I feel the needle in my thigh, then a burning sensation that spreads up and down my leg, into my stomach, arms, and my feet. Going limp, the last thing I remember is Mary holding one hand and the little girl holding the other.

They're screaming. "Don't forget!"

I wake on the floor. Everything is foggy.

Where am I? My cheek is pressed to the concrete, and as I sit up, a line of drool falls down my chin.

There's something I'm supposed to remember. I'm sure I knew it once.

Looking around, I realize I'm in seclusion. How did I get here? I have no idea.

What is the last thing I remember? I'm drawing a blank. Wasn't someone with me? I get a momentary flash, but it's my roommate, Mary.

That doesn't make sense. She doesn't even talk.

How long have I been here?

I hear the door start to creak open, so I turn toward the noise. It's Doctor… Doctor… Hank? No, that's not right. Doctor… Herbert. Doctor Herbert. I remember. There's someone behind him. Who is that? They're blurry; I can't quite make them out.

He gives me a stern look. "Nadia, what were you doing out of your room in the middle of the night?"

"What?" I have no idea what he's talking about. Wouldn't I have been sleeping?

He shifts to his other foot, seeming irritated. "Why were you out of bed and in the hallway in the middle of the night?"

"I… I don't know, Dr. Herbert. I don't remember doing that." This is the truth. I don't have any recollection of anything before seclusion.

The blurry person behind him steps forward. "We found these in her room, Doctor." They're holding some sheets of paper. I don't know what they are.

Dr. Herbert begins reading the sheets, and a look of shock crosses his face. "Are these yours, Nadia?"

I glance at the sheets, but they don't look familiar to me. "I don't think so, Dr. Herbert."

"Doctor, they were found in her drawer. With her sketches."

Sketches? My sketches? Do I draw?

Dr. Herbert reddens and begins writing in my chart, speaking to the blurry person. "Prep the procedure room. We're going to nip this in the bud right now. A round of ECT should clear her head."

ECT? That's not shock therapy. Is it? I don't want that. I start to protest, then remember that it's not a good idea to argue. Bad things happen when you don't do what you're told.

Pacing around the seclusion room, I wonder again how I got here. I'm foggy but agitated. Something is wrong, very wrong.

I'm supposed to remember.

What am I supposed to remember?

I sit on the cot and give the thin mattress a good punch. Looking over at the door, I see the little girl in her green velvet dress.

Groaning, I ask, "What do you want?" She only shows up when my meds are wearing off, and I'm too frustrated to deal with her right now.

"I'm here to remind you. You know that."

"If you're here to remind me, then why aren't you reminding me?!" I scream at her. I pick up the mattress and throw it, but it falls a foot away, limp.

"You have to stay calm. You can't force it. But you can remember. I know you can." She sits down near the mattress, cross-legged.

I'm angry now. I'm tired, frustrated, foggy, and confused. I know she isn't real, but I'm so mad, I swipe at her. When I connect, and my fingers brush her soft cheek, I stagger back. Now I'm also frightened.

"What's going on?"

She stands and walks over, putting her small arms around my waist, hugging me. "It's going to be okay. We can get through this."

Not knowing what to do, I hug her back. I close my eyes.

There's a small flicker. I see Mary's face.

I open them again and look down at the girl. She's looking up at me with her large, green eyes open wide. She nods.

Another flicker comes. I can feel the truth pushing through my brain, trying to surface. I'm on the precipice of remembering.

I hear a squeaking noise, and the door swings open. Two orderlies walk through, each taking an arm.

"No!" I scream. "You can't!" The flicker in my brain has become a small spark. I know that if I can kindle it, I'll remember.

I stop fighting and go limp in their arms. If they want to take me somewhere else, they can drag me.

I focus all my energy on my breath. The little girl is walking beside me, holding my hand.

I stopped taking my pills. I remember. Why?

Suddenly, Mary is on my other side, holding my other hand. Why is Mary here?

Like a bolt of lightning, all the dots connect. The flame grows. It consumes the fogginess, frustration, anger, and doubt.

I remember.

"I remember!" Mary and the little girl both light up, ecstatic that I did it. That *we* did it.

The orderlies look at me like I'm crazy.

It's okay, I am crazy. But I remember.

Mary, the little girl, and I did it. They can't break us with meds anymore. As hard as they've tried, they can't break me.

While being dragged through the hallway, I see the sun rising out of the large windows on the other side of the nurses' station.

I smile. It's a good omen.

"I agree," Mary says. She still clasps my hand tightly.

We're in the procedure room now, strapped to the table.

Well, I am. Mary and the little girl are standing by my side, looking frightened and sad.

All I can really see are the bright overhead lights. I hear them humming. A nurse is bustling around, the fabric of her dress rustling. There's clanking as metal tools are spread out on a tray. The smell of alcohol and antiseptic stings my nose and throat.

I'm cold, and my foot itches.

The nurse starts an IV, and it pinches for just a second.

Mary squeezes my hand.

Suddenly, a face is hovering over me. Nurse Delaney. She looks worn and angry. There are lines around her eyes and mouth that I don't remember being there. She's haggard in a way that she wasn't before.

Before what? Before, here?

Suddenly, I remember. "I know you."

Incredulity registers on her face. "We need to get her anesthesia in, NOW! She's too lucid." She turns away in a hurry.

I turn to Mary and the little girl. "I know her."

"We know." Mary pats my hand. "It's okay."

The little girl has tears in her eyes. "It's going to be okay. They can't keep us separated, no matter how many times they try."

Mary nods. "You've done so well. We'll make it back, I know it."

There's a coolness sliding up my arm. I can feel it spread over my body, and somehow, the coolness warms me. The world seems to dim. Sounds grow quieter, and the lights start to fade.

The last thing I see is Mary and the little girl. They're talking, but I can't hear them.

I try to stay conscious, but everything fades to black.

Thirty-Two

Waking up, I'm confused.

Where am I?

There's a nurse moving around near my bed.

I look down. There's an IV in my arm. Startled, I try to sit up, but a wave of nausea hits me like a truck. My head hurts from the slightest movement.

The nurse rushes over. "It's okay, hon. You're okay. Don't try to sit up yet."

"Where am I?" I mumble, but what comes out doesn't sound like words. It's more of a gurgle.

"Shhhh, it's okay. You're okay. You're in the recovery ward." She fluffs my pillow and grabs a blood pressure cuff and stethoscope. After checking my vitals, she gives me more information. "You had a small procedure, but you're fine. By tomorrow you'll be right as rain and ready to go back to your room, and by the day after you can resume normal activities."

What are normal activities? My room? Do I live here? I don't understand what is going on.

The exertion of waking up and having a one-sided conversation is too much right now, and I fall asleep just as confused as I had woken up.

The next few hours are spent waking, then sleeping again. Waking and sleeping. Each time I wake, I'm disoriented and have to be told where I am. By the sixth or seventh time I wake up, I finally remember that I'm in the recovery ward. I don't know what that means, but I know the nurse has said it a couple of times before.

This time, I find that even though my words are a little mushy, they're understandable. "Excuse me?"

The nurse comes over and hands me a glass of water. "Yes, hon? Do you need something?" She seems nice. Gentle.

"I'm sorry, but… where am I? I don't remember." I look at her, hopeful that she knows something that can help me understand what's going on.

"Oh, dear. Hon, you're at Ravensbrook Institute. You have a history of…" She checks the chart hanging off the end of the bed. "Manic-depressive psychosis." She looks at me, seeing how I'm taking this information.

"Oh. I didn't know that." I'm in a loony bin? How long have I been here?

I realize I don't have any memories. Horrified, I ask another question.

"Do… Do you know my name?"

She looks at me sympathetically. "Your name is Nadia, hon."

"Nadia. Okay, thank you." It's not a weird name, but it feels strange on my tongue. Like it belongs to someone else.

I think hard. How can a person have no memories? There has to be *something* I remember. Looking at my hands and down at my body, I know I'm an adult. A woman.

A woman named Nadia.

Well, that's a start, I guess.

The nice nurse in recovery keeps me overnight again to monitor my blood pressure and temperature. She tells me I had shock therapy, which is why I'm in the recovery ward. It was to control my outbursts and calm me.

It must have worked; I feel pretty calm. I have a follow-up question. "Excuse me?"

She turns. "Yes, hon?"

"If I'm in a mental institution, do I normally take some sort of medication?" I've been lucid long enough to understand that I haven't taken anything while here.

"Well, you're normally on Thorazine, but you won't start it again until you go back to your normal room. We like to be able to monitor patients' vitals without competing with medication during recovery." She looks to see if this satisfies my curiosity.

It does. "Thank you. Sorry for the twenty questions."

She smiles. "No problem at all. I know it's hard to wake up and not remember everything."

It's not everything that I don't remember. It's anything.

The next afternoon, she wheels me to my room. The number on the door is 108. I'll have to remember that, so I know how to get back if I leave.

Stepping into the room, I see I have two roommates. One of them is lying down on her bed, just inside the door. The other is sitting on her bed, which lines the adjacent wall. She's staring into space and doesn't seem to notice that I'm here.

I turn to thank the nurse, and she hands me a small paper cup of water. Thanking her, I take my pill and lie down on what I assume is my bed. It's the only other one that has a pillow.

I fall asleep easily. Waking sometime later, the women are gone, and I'm alone in the room. I feel strange. Foggy. Like all the sharp edges on things are blurred and squishy.

Sitting up, I rub my eyes. They feel gritty.

Where am I again? That's right. The nut house. I wonder where the other women went. Looking over at the bureau, there's a tray of food that's been left. It must be for me.

Getting out of bed, I need a moment to get my bearings. Standing up made me a little lightheaded.

I try to walk over to the tray, but I have a hard time lifting my feet to move. I try shuffling. That works fine. Picking the tray up, I shuffle back to bed.

I stab a piece of meat with the fork. It's slimy. My stomach turns. Nothing on the tray looks remotely edible. Putting it back on the bureau, I shuffle back to bed and stare at the ceiling.

Is this really my life?

I see the sun starting to set out the window, and the room darkens. The fluorescent lights hum. They're too bright.

Getting up again, I explore the small room. It's just six beds and a dresser, with a window that's sealed shut.

I open a drawer in the dresser, wondering which is mine. After closing it, I notice that labels are haphazardly stuck in the top-right corner of each drawer. Bending down, I see one labeled 'Nadia.' The writing doesn't look fresh.

For the first time, I wonder how long I've been here.

Opening my drawer, there are shirts, pants, underwear, socks, and an extra robe. There's a pair of slippers by my bed. There's nothing personal here. No photos or mementos to give me a clue as to who I was or what my life was like before coming here.

As I'm staring into my drawer, frowning, the door opens. In walks two women, one behind the other. Their outlines are blurry, and I can't really see their faces. The first sits on the bed two down from mine, along the same wall. The other sits on the last bed on the adjacent wall.

"Hello," I say to the woman two beds down.

She smiles at me demurely. "Hi, Nadia. How are you feeling?"

I'm confused. She knows me? "I'm sorry, do I know you?"

She looks sad. "Yes. I'm Judy. We've been roommates for months now."

"Oh, sorry." I didn't mean to hurt her feelings. "I think I had ECT, so my memory is a little foggy."

"It's okay." She lies down on her bed, staring at the ceiling. "I think we all have a touch of mental problems."

I look to the woman in the adjacent bed. "Hi," I call to her.

She doesn't answer.

I look over to Judy, and she's smiling at me. "I'm glad you didn't lose her."

"Uh, okay." This woman is obviously not fine.

A nurse comes in with evening rounds. She starts with Judy.

That seems weird. I'm already foggy and confused. They're giving me more meds?

The nurse comes over to me next. She's got dark, curly hair and is wearing a dainty necklace. I think it's a cross, but it's blurry, so I can't tell.

"Excuse me?" I take the paper cup from her, but I want to ask first if this is right.

"Yes, hon, how can I help you?" She smiles at me. She seems nice.

"Um, I don't know if I'm due for meds again yet. I'm feeling really foggy and off-balance." Maybe she just didn't know I had meds before lunch.

"This is the right dose, dear. Dr. Herbert has upped it since your last outburst." She hands me a small cup of water.

"I'm not sure…" I start, but she interrupts me.

"Nadia, take your meds." She sounds stern now. "You don't want to end up in seclusion, do you?" Her smile is gone, and her voice sounds commanding.

"Oh, okay. No, I don't want to get in trouble." I take the pill and swallow it with the water, then hand back the cups.

She's still standing in front of me. What is she waiting for?

"Well?" She taps her foot impatiently.

"I… I'm sorry. What am I supposed to be doing?"

She grabs my face and forces my mouth open, checking under my tongue and inside my cheeks. Then she lets go as if I disgust her. "You know you're supposed to show me that you swallowed it." She sounds angry.

"I… I'm sorry, Nurse…" I realize I don't know her.

She calms quickly. So quickly, it feels fake. Forced. "Sorry, dear. I forget sometimes that memory can be sticky after ECT. I'm Nurse Delaney. I'll try to be more patient next time."

She leaves the room without going to the bed of the third woman.

How strange.

Thirty-Three

I wake in the morning foggy and lightheaded. A nurse comes in and gives me another dose. I try to tell her that my meds are already too strong, that I don't need another dose, but all it earns me is a needle in the thigh and a morning in seclusion.

I don't like seclusion. It's hard to be alone with your thoughts when you don't really have thoughts. No past to think about, nothing going on at present, and seemingly no future.

Is this all there is? I want to cry, but I'm so numb I don't think I can.

Realizing I have to pee, I look around. There's nowhere to relieve yourself. I'm not sure what to do; I really have to go. I came here right after waking up, so I haven't gone since yesterday.

Just then, the door creaks and swings open.

At least something is going in my favor today.

Instead of someone taking me out, a man steps in. He's wearing a long white coat and carrying a stethoscope. There's an upside-down heart-shaped birthmark on his cheek. I try not to look at it. It's unsettling.

"Hi, Nadia," he starts. He riffles through some pages in my chart, then looks up. "How are you feeling?"

"I really need to pee," I tell him.

He closes the door behind him. "Well, that's going to have to wait until we have a chat."

"Okay," I say softly. I can see that arguing doesn't do any good here. I have to try my best to hold it.

"The nurses tell me you're complaining about your meds." He looks stoic and formidable.

"Um, well, I—" I start. All I can think about is relieving myself. There not being a place to do it intensifies the need. "I just… I feel so foggy, and my mind is mushy. I'm numb. I don't remember anything, even what I did yesterday."

He nods. "That sounds normal. I don't think your dose is too high; you just need to adjust." Making a note in my chart, he asks another question. "So, you don't remember anything prior to yesterday?"

I'm squirming now. "I, uh, I don't think I remember anything from before coming to this room. Can I go pee now?"

He seems satisfied with my answer to his question, but doesn't answer mine. His pen moves across my chart, adding additional notes. "We're going to keep you at your current dosage for now. I'll have an orderly come in to take you to the bathroom and then back to…" He stops speaking as he sees the look on my face.

It's too late. I can feel the warmth running down my legs, soaking my pants and my slippers. It starts to pool at my feet. I held it as long as I could.

"I'm sorry," I whisper to the doctor. I just pissed myself in front of him, and I don't even know his name.

His face shows how disgusted he is, and as the smell of urine hits him, he backs up to the door and exits, slamming it behind him.

I strip my pants, underwear, socks, and slippers off and place them in a pile near the door. Only then do I notice the drain in the center of the room. That would have been helpful ten minutes ago.

More time goes by. I'm not sure how long, but longer than if the doctor had sent an orderly to take me to the bathroom and back to my room.

I'm cold and sticky. Is this a punishment for not being able to hold it longer? I'm learning quickly that you have to do what you're told. The consequences aren't worth fighting it.

Time continues passing, and eventually the door opens again. It's an orderly with a tray of food. He leaves clean clothes and picks up the dirty ones, giving me a disgusted look before closing the door behind him.

Punishment, it is.

He didn't give me anything to clean myself with. I feel less than human as I put on the new clothes over the dried urine.

The only small miracle is that they haven't given me another dose of meds. I think between the doctor's disgust and me being in seclusion, someone forgot.

I eat what I can from the tray, thinking that maybe the food can soak up some of the medicine.

Sitting on the cot, I figure it must be time to nap. I'm not sure how long I've been in here, but it's long enough that I'm tired again. Lying down, the cot smells faintly of urine. Hopefully, it's just the smell of my own stuck in my nose.

Twice more today, I use the drain as a toilet. It makes me feel gross, but less gross than my accident did. I won't make that mistake again.

Eventually, the door swings open, and an orderly comes in to take me back to my room. I'm glad to be out of seclusion. The cot on the floor is uncomfortable, and my mind isn't right enough to be alone with my thoughts.

Except I have no thoughts.

Thirty-Four

It's dark outside, so I must have spent the whole day alone. My meds have worn off somewhat, and I feel marginally better. I wish I didn't have to take more soon. Don't some people skip meds? How do they do it? If the nurses are checking, how do they not see?

I'm lying in bed. Judy is too.

The other roommate is staring off into nothing. I stare at her for a little while, wondering what's going on with her. The nurse ignored her, and Judy acted weird when I said hello.

I sense movement on my other side, in one of the empty beds. Turning quickly, I'm really hoping it isn't a rat. I hate rats.

I'm shocked when I see a little girl. She's a beautiful child, probably six or seven years old. Blonde hair, plaited down her back. She's wearing a green velvet dress, the kind you put your kids in for the holidays. There's a matching bow on top of her head.

I blink. This can't be real. I turn to Judy and roommate #2, but neither of them seems to see her.

The little girl looks at me. "You're not wrong. People do skip meds. You could do it, too." She looks back down at the book she's reading.

"H-how did you know what I was thinking?" I'm trembling. Is she a mind reader? A ghost?

"No, I'm not a ghost," she says, putting down her book. "I'm here to remind you. You know that."

"I do?" I look over, and Judy is watching me, but she doesn't say anything. She smiles and then turns back to staring at the ceiling.

The other woman doesn't acknowledge me.

"What are you here to remind me about?" Have I seen her before? If she thinks I know what she's talking about, I must have.

"I can't tell you that, silly. You need to remember." She bounces slightly on the bed. "This bed isn't very springy."

This must be the psychosis they keep telling me I have. I see people who don't exist.

"You said I could skip pills. How do I do that? I don't like the meds. They make everything taste bad and make everyone blurry." Maybe she knows how to do it.

"You've done it before."

I have? She seems to know more about me than I do. Can I trust this little girl who isn't real? What if she's a delusion and my mind is trying to hurt me? Why would the doctors and nurses all lie to me and tell me I need the meds if I don't?

"I don't know. I have no idea what to think." I'm scared and confused.

She leans over. "It's okay. We're going to get through this. When the nurse comes in, pretend to take the pill. Move it into your upper lip and then show them your empty mouth. Easy peasy." She sounds like she knows what she's talking about.

I'm going to try. I don't want more meds.

The nurse comes in for rounds, and I don't think she's someone I've seen before. Not the same woman from this morning who got mad and stabbed me in the leg with the needle. I know I told the doctor that I didn't remember anything from before seclusion, but I had to pee so bad I couldn't think straight. I do remember a little from today and even slightly from last night. I remember a nurse wearing a dainty cross on a chain.

"Hold on to that." The little girl looks excited. "It's important."

"How is a cross important?" I ask her.

"It just is. Look!" She points to my other roommate, who is now looking at me.

"Oh, hi," I say shyly. I'm worried she's going to think I'm crazy for talking to myself. Then I remember we're all in here for more or less the same reasons.

"Hi," she says quietly. She turns back and resumes staring into space.

"You're doing it!" The little girl shouts. She's ecstatic.

I don't understand.

The nurse asks if I'm okay. She heard me talking to myself.

"Oh, yes, I'm fine. Thank you." I smile at her, but I can feel one side of my mouth droop. My smile must be lopsided.

She hands me the paper cup and the water. I put the pill in my mouth, then pretend to swig it back with the water, moving it into my upper lip. Smiling at the nurse, I open my mouth so she can check that I took it.

Looking satisfied, she takes the paper cup and the water back from me and leaves. She skips my other roommate, just like the nurse yesterday.

That's really confusing.

I look over, and the little girl is doing cartwheels, her dress fanning out around her as she spins. "You did it!"

"I did!" I say, taking the pill out of my mouth. "Gross, this tastes terrible." I look around, wondering what I'm supposed to do with it.

The little girl is looking at me intently.

"What?" I'm not sure why she's staring at me.

"There's something you're supposed to remember."

I sigh. "There are a lot of things I'm sure I'm supposed to remember, but I don't." I'm still holding the small pill in my palm.

"Yes, but you already remembered some of it. You remembered that you've skipped pills before." She looks on edge, as if she isn't sure whether I'm going to grasp what she's saying.

"No, *you* told me I've done it before."

"Exactly." She looks at me as if I've just solved a riddle.

What is she talking about? And where am I going to put this pill?

Then it dawns on me.

"Wait, are you me? I mean, obviously, you're not me, but you're in my brain, so you know things that I don't? Are you part of me that I can't reach on my own because of this place?"

She stands on the bed and starts doing a happy little dance, hands swinging through the air.

I laugh. The pill is still in my hand. "Okay, smarty-pants. If you know what I've done before, what did I do with the other pills I supposedly didn't take?"

She stops dancing and looks at my other roommate. "Mary knows."

Mary? Is that her name? Why would she know what I've done with other pills? Do I trust her? I'm learning very quickly not to trust anyone here. But I do trust the little girl.

"Mary?" I say out loud. There's a flicker in my head. The ECT and meds have dulled my senses, but instinct tells me they aren't gone. Just buried.

Mary looks at me, a small smile on her face. "Nadia," she says back.

I'm still missing something. What is it? I knew once; I know I did.

"Um, where do I put this?" I ask Mary.

She gets out of bed and comes to sit next to the little girl on the bed next to mine. They look at each other and smile.

She sees her?

Mary turns back to me. "You know where to put the pill."

I'm frustrated. "I don't!" Why are they toying with me? How can Mary see the little girl?

The little girl looks at me. "Relax. Don't try too hard. Trying too hard makes the memories go away; it doesn't bring them back."

"How am I supposed to relax? I have no idea what's going on!" I don't know how to do what she's asking of me.

She takes my hand. "Take a deep breath. Now."

I'm shaking, but I close my eyes and try to steady my breathing. All of this is happening fast, and my brain is still scrambled.

"Focus. It's okay. You're getting it." The little girl speaks quietly. Soothingly.

I try to focus on the flicker in my head. Breathing slowly, I feel the little girl squeeze my hand. Then, I feel my other hand being taken.

I open my eyes, and Mary is looking at me and holding my hand.

The flicker flares, sputtering. Sparks of memories are flying around inside my head like a million tiny fireflies.

My eyes go wide. I rip my hands from theirs and start searching the seam of the mattress with my fingertips. I feel along until I come to a tiny opening. Feeling underneath, I find the bottom side of the safety pin holding it together.

The sparks are starting to catch fire. I'm doing it.

Unclasping the pin, I pull apart the unstitched seam of the mattress and plunge my fingers inside. I pull back two sheets of paper and a cup full of pills.

I look at the other two, shocked.

The fire in my mind is roaring now, and tears spring to my eyes as I lean forward and hug them.

"We did it," I whisper. "We made it out again."

"I knew you could," Mary whispers back. She and the little girl are both crying, too.

"You know, my brain separating us was the smartest thing I ever did. We couldn't have done it without all three of us."

I lie back on the bed, a little sweaty, but so grateful to have my memory back.

They tried so hard to silence me. But there's something they didn't count on.

We are not going out without a fight.

Thirty-Five

I sleep like a baby. In the morning, I'm refreshed, if a little hungover. There are new plans to make now.

I skip the morning pill with ease, putting on my lopsided smile act.

At lunch, Delaney comes over to see if I have any interest in drawing portraits, and I feign shock that I know how to draw.

You see, I don't remember drawing portraits. I've never drawn them, as far as I know.

Nurse Delaney looks annoyed, but tells me that I am indeed wonderful at portraits, and she'll check back in a few days to see how I'm feeling about it.

As she leaves, Mary, the little girl, and I laugh at her expense.

She turns around and looks at me like I'm crazy.

It's ok. I am. I'm crazy but also mentally strong. Two things can be true.

After dinner, I sit in the activity room sketching. Since Delaney is here today, I don't sketch anyone I know. She needs to think that I remember absolutely nothing. I draw celebrities. Mary Tyler Moore, Burt Reynolds, and Jane Fonda appear in front of me.

Delaney slinks by and stops short. "Oh, Nadia! You remembered that you can draw?" She picks up the drawing of Burt Reynolds. "These are great!"

I look foggy and give her my lopsided smile. "Thank you! I just copied them out of this magazine," I hold up a

TV Guide. "I wouldn't say I remembered so much as my hands just kind of put these pictures on the paper." I grin at her as foolishly as I can, going slightly cross-eyed.

She puts the paper down and looks slightly unsettled. "That's great, Nadia. Good work." Then she hurries away.

This is going well. I need her to think she's broken me; that my brain no longer works.

After evening rounds, I'm lying in bed with the others on either side. I've recovered everything I lost. At least, to the best of my knowledge. All the notes I took and the copies I made were helpful.

Stealing the safety pin from Delaney's desk during one of my portrait sessions in her office was the most genius move I've ever made. And then unstitching the seam of the mattress? It was Mary's idea, but it was perfection.

"So," Mary says quietly, picking at a nail. "Now what?"

I turn my head to look at her. "There's still planning to do. If we don't execute it perfectly next time, we won't get another chance."

She nods. "If you're caught again, there won't be a next time."

Hearing it out loud sends a chill down my spine.

There's a whirring sound, and then a click, and the lights go out. That's fine, I do some of my best thinking in the dark.

"Have you tried searching for more memories?" the little girl asks. It seems to come from nowhere, but it must have been on my mind.

I haven't. I've been mostly trying to solidify the best possible plan to get everyone out of here. I brush her hair out of her face and then pinch her cheek.

"Ow! What was that for?"

I laugh. "Nothing, you're just cute, that's all."

She pouts. "I'm not cute. I'm big." She looks at me hard, waiting for me to apologize.

"I'm sorry." I chuckle. "You're right. You're the biggest help in the whole world." She genuinely is. She brought me back. She brought Mary back.

Her smile returns, and she basks in the praise.

"I haven't thought about it. But obviously you have."

"I think it's time," she says.

I would love a new memory. I don't know how to unlock them easily; they seem to appear almost at random. "How do I make them happen?" I ask her.

"You don't," Mary chimes in. "You *let* them happen." She sits up on the bed, cross-legged. "Try lying down and just clearing your mind completely. You're always thinking too hard; it's why they don't just resurface."

She's right. When I'm lucid, my mind is constantly whirring, trying to figure out what's next.

I lay my head down and close my eyes. Picturing only darkness, I don't let thoughts creep into my head. Suddenly, I feel it. It's pushing on my brain, trying to push *through* my brain. Taking another deep breath, I don't rush it.

I see him. Dark hair, glasses, handsome in a way that takes my breath away. He looks serious.

What is he saying? I can't make out the words, but he's upset.

My mouth is dry, but my eyes are not.

He stands up, and I can smell a hint of his cologne. He smells like cedar and tobacco.

Putting his ring on the table, it spins, then wobbles for a second as I hear it trying to settle.

When I look up, he's walking out the door. All that's left is the ring on the table and the lingering smell of him.

I bolt up and unpin the mattress, ripping the pages out of it and flying through them, looking for him. I come to a portrait I drew at least a week ago. There he is. Handsome in a studious way. A smirk on his face and just the right amount of laugh lines around his eyes. I captured him perfectly. Good-natured, intelligent, and slightly silly.

My eyes fill with tears.

He left me.

He left because I came here.

My husband left me.

I'm breathing fast.

"Did you know?" I ask them. "Did you?" My heart is beating out of my chest. I loved him. And he left because I'm crazy.

"No," they both say.

Mary adds, "We only know what you know. I'm so sorry, Nadia." She hugs me, and I collapse into her, sobbing.

Maybe I didn't want this memory. Couldn't this have been the one that didn't return? I would have liked that more.

I cry into Mary's shoulder, and the little girl grasps my hand quietly. Neither of them can help, and they know it.

My breath shudders, even as the tears start to dry up.

I loved him. And he left. I was too much; my illness was something we couldn't conquer together.

My heart breaks all over again.

Eventually, my breath evens, and I fall asleep in Mary's arms, the little girl curled into my chest. I know it's bad to be psychotic, but here, loneliness is worse.

The next morning, I'm still heartbroken. I drift through breakfast, OT, and lunch, feeling sorry for myself. During quiet time, I lay listlessly in bed. Mary is back on her own bed, and the little girl is curled up beside her. They're giving me the time I need to grieve.

Putting my hand to my face, I want to shut out the world. Lying on my pillow, staring at the ceiling, I put two pieces together.

I look over, but Mary and the little girl already know.

I have to say it out loud. That's how I'll know it's true. I don't get up, but I tell them, "The first memory, the one that I confused for Vic. It was my husband."

The little girl comes over and tentatively sits next to me. "It's okay. You remembered, that's what's important."

"It's not the only thing that's important!" I know she's trying to help, but my emotions are raw now. "My mind is so fucked that I confused my brother for my husband in a memory. I'm sick."

"It makes sense," Mary tells me. "They're two men you trusted. And you knew about Vic first."

If nothing else, at least that memory is straightened out.

Thirty-Six

I take another day to drift endlessly in a deep pool of emotions before I've licked my wounds enough to push forward.

Knowing that he left because I'm broken hurts, but the more I think about it, the more it makes me want to burn this place to the ground. It seems to be a catch-all for my shattered dreams.

Before I remembered him, I spent days planning how to get back to the records room. They don't leave my door unlocked anymore. Even if it does happen accidentally, someone always comes by to check and lock it back up.

So this time, I need to rely on a solid plan rather than luck.

At breakfast, Delaney approaches me about drawing. I smile my sweet, lopsided smile at her and act foggy, as if I don't know what she wants from me.

She tells me she'll get me when it's time for OT, and we can talk again.

I can handle another few days of portraits. After consulting my list of nurses' shifts earlier, it seems tonight is a prime evening to execute my plan. If not tonight, I'll likely have to wait another week for the stars to align. That's not something I'm willing to do.

During OT, I sit in Delaney's office and draw for the nurses. Briefly, I go through her desk to see if there's anything that might be helpful, but there's nothing.

I wonder when I'll figure out who I was before this place. Have I ever figured it out before?

Thinking again about my file, sitting there in the cabinet drawer with everyone else's, I can't help but daydream that maybe the missing pieces can be found there.

The rest of the day trudges by, each minute feeling like an hour. Part of me doesn't want tonight to come. Maybe I'm not brave enough, or smart enough, to pull it off. But the other part of me wants to get it over with. The part that knows what I would lose by staying: what any of us could lose.

I've been on high alert today each time I pass by the nurses' station. The right opportunity needs to present itself, or the rest of the plan is useless.

During activity time, I take a break from sketching for the nurses and let my hand and mind wander.

The hurt surrounding my husband is still fresh, but it's now more like a dark bruise than a knife wound. Putting my pencil to the paper, his brow, chin, and the hollow of his throat appear. A tear falls on the page as his eyes come to life. His short hair. It was too fluffy to let it grow longer. A small scar by his mouth. He'd told me that he fell off a bike as a kid and needed a few stitches.

When the portrait is done, I hold it back and admire it.

He was beautiful. I loved him. And he's gone now.

All of those things are true.

I go back to sketching for Delaney, but my heart isn't in it.

Finally, on the way back to 108 post-dinner, I get my chance. Someone threw up in the hallway near the activity room, so all the staff are in that wing trying to clean it up while keeping the half-awake patients from stepping in it.

I know another patient could see me, but I'm less worried about that. Everyone is so doped up that even if they do notice, they won't care. And even if they care, they won't remember in thirty minutes.

Slipping into the nurses' station, I implement phases one and two. First, I hurry over to the coffeepot. Taking the small, rolled-up paper cup out of my shoe, I dump the crushed pills into the water tank. There are two weeks of pills in there, at least. I'm hoping it knocks them all out for at least a couple of hours. Between the nurses adding water and the coffee's heat, they should dissolve beautifully.

After checking the hall to make sure there are no staff in sight, I swipe the keyring that hangs on the hook by the desk. There's a chance someone could notice they're missing, but I don't think they will. The doors all lock from the outside, and the staff don't really use them. The rooms are more like cages, and the keys are ornamental.

Rushing back into the hall, there are still no staff around.

I did it.

I'm sweating, and my mouth is dry, but I managed to pull off the first step of my plan.

Stepping into 108, I rush over and fall into bed. I was terrified I'd be caught, but I made it.

Mary smiles at me. "You really nailed that. Flawless."

I smile back at her. "Let's hope it's a sign that the rest of the night goes just as well."

The little girl hugs me. "You're going to do great. I just know it."

I cross my fingers. "Now we wait. I've been waiting and watching for weeks, and they brew their coffee after lights out." Curling up on the pillow, I add, "We should be able to smell it shortly after dark."

Being right down the hall from the nurses' station is a blessing in this case.

As much as today dragged, the minutes tick by like molasses running down a wall tonight.

I'm jumpy.

My nerves are shot.

I keep looking at the other two, but we don't speak anymore. There's really nothing else to say.

Finally, I hear the click, and we're plunged into darkness. The antiseptic smell is extra strong tonight. Whether that's real or imagined, I can't be sure.

What feels like hours, but is probably closer to twenty minutes later, we can smell the coffee brewing.

Judy 1 is long asleep. Sleeping and eating are about all she does these days, unless she's propped up in front of the TV in the activity room watching sitcom reruns.

Mary looks at me, wide-eyed. "Is it time?"

"Not yet. We need to give it time and make sure that they all get their chance for a pick-me-up, and it's had time to kick in." The last thing I need is to rush this and have an orderly late to tonight's coffee party.

She nods. It's the right thing to do, hard as it is.

I bide my time trying different keys in the door. They aren't marked, so it takes a while to find the one for 108. In reality, this keyring is useless. In an emergency, you wouldn't have that long to test each key.

I wasn't wrong, thinking it's ornamental.

Gauging time in here is hard, but I wait what reasonably seems like forty-five minutes to an hour.

It's time.

Thirty-Seven

I unlock the door and step out into the hallway, putting the keyring in my robe pocket. I'm on high alert for any noise, but hear nothing.

As I start to move, the keys jingle.

Shit.

Holding the keys to my thigh, I begin my very slow descent down the hall to the nurses' station, stopping every few yards to listen.

Making my way to the column, I stop and wait. The only sounds are the clock ticking on the wall and a desk fan oscillating.

The smell of coffee is strong.

Peering around the column, two nurses are sitting hunched over and asleep on the desktop. One of them still has a pen in hand, as if she fell asleep mid-paperwork.

This gives me a small amount of confidence, so I step out from behind the column a bit. I need to make sure the night orderlies are out cold, too. I hear nothing except the desk fan and the clock.

As I walk around the desk, I intend to put the keyring back where I found it. Before I make it, I trip and fall onto the floor, knocking over a wastebasket. It clangs on the linoleum flooring.

SHIT.

I scramble up, hiding as best I can between the nurse's chairs.

My heart is in my throat. It's beating so fast it feels like it may burst.

A moment passes.

Then two.

Nobody comes.

I breathe a shaky sigh of relief and stand up. Peeking around the desk, I'm curious what I tripped over.

It's an orderly, passed out on the floor by the nurse's desk.

Wow. I literally tripped over him without waking him up. That's a great sign.

For my own mental peace, I need to know where the last orderly is.

Sneaking back into the hall, I quietly cross the extra yards to the procedure room.

It's dark.

I open the door, to be sure.

Nobody is there.

I breathe another sigh of relief, thankful that there were no surgeries planned for tonight.

I'm not sure where else to look for the other orderly, and I don't want to waste time; I could be grabbing the files. I don't know for sure how long the pills will keep everyone asleep.

I quietly walk back to the nurses' station and over to the records room.

The door is ajar.

Turning on the light, I groan inwardly.

I found the last orderly.

He's asleep on the floor right in front of the two cabinets I need.

I really hope he stays asleep, because this is my shot.

My heart races as I straddle his body to get to Judy 2's file, and my own, in the *Research Studies* cabinet. As quietly as I can, I remove it and close the drawer.

He lets out a snore.

I nearly jump out of my skin.

Thankfully, he's still very asleep.

I turn to the *Patient Outcomes* drawer, taking Judy's file, my file, and the *Grant Money – Seeds* file. I manage to close this drawer just as silently.

Stepping back over the orderly and out into the nurses' station, I let out a shaky breath.

Taking three steps over to the sleeping nurses, I reach over one of them to grab the Scotch tape.

As quickly as possible, I'm back out into the hallway and walking down the corridor, away from 108. I keep stopping to listen, but there's nothing. The further I get from the nurses' station, the more this place feels like a tomb.

The deadly quiet is eerie.

Finally, after what feels like hours, I make it to my destination.

The visitors' lounge.

This door isn't locked. There's no need for it.

I step inside and close the door quietly behind me. Not wanting to turn on the light, I wait a moment and let my eyes adjust. There's just enough moonlight that I can see the outlines of the chairs and tables.

Creeping over to the corner table where Vic always is, I sit on the floor. Nesting Judy 2's files and the Grant Money files into one folder, I tape the edges so nothing can fall out. Then, lying under the table, I tape the whole package there, widthwise and lengthwise, to make sure it will stay.

I know Vic will be back either tomorrow or the next day, but I don't want to take any chances.

Standing up, I wipe my hands on my pants. I'm a little shaky, but proud of what I've accomplished.

The last piece is just returning the tape on my way back to 108. As long as everyone is still asleep, this should be the easiest part of the journey, though I have a hard time convincing myself it will be.

Stepping out into the hall, I'm pretty confident that everyone is still out cold. There were a LOT of pills to crush up.

Really, they should be asleep for hours.

Walking back to the room, I'm less anxious than I've been in weeks. I stick to the side of the hallway as a precaution, but it's probably overkill.

Dropping the tape dispenser back on the nurse's desk on my way by, I stop after the column to slow my racing heart.

Then I hear them.

Footsteps.

My breath catches in my throat. I look down the hall towards my room. There's nobody there. The footsteps must be coming from the other way.

It's so quiet otherwise that I can hear a conversation drifting down the hallway. I recognize the voices instantly.

"Who do we have tonight, Nurse?"

Dr. Herbert is here.

Why is he here?

Then I realize my miscalculation.

This is much earlier than I've snuck out before. I've only ever heard the screams late at night. They don't begin right after lights out.

Delaney answers him. "Marlene Chabot." I hear papers rustle. "We have her scheduled for an amygdalotomy."

They're talking in the open about their illegal surgeries like they're out for a walk on a spring day, just discussing the weather.

The absolute gall.

They're so used to being above the law, it's no big deal. Ruining people's lives, their futures, is just another night at work for them.

I clasp the two remaining files tightly. My face is hot, and I'm sweating, but it's not from anxiety anymore.

Anger fuels me, and I can't wait to take these fuckers down.

I peer around the column. The doctor and nurse are nearly at the station. They take a few more steps and then stop, stock-still.

"What on earth is going on here?" Doctor Herbert looks confused.

Delaney is outraged. "Why are you asleep?!" she screams at the two nurses. She grabs one and shakes her awake, but only for a moment. The nurse turns and vomits all over Delaney's bright white uniform, and she steps back in disgust. The sickly nurse crumples to the floor and passes out again.

Smiling, I know I've seen enough.

They'll have their hands full for the rest of the night with the staff who have come down with an unknown sickness.

Staying against the wall, I creep the rest of the way back to 108.

Locking the door, I shut it behind me.

It's far too dark to read anything in the folders, so I hide them under my mattress. Nobody will be looking for them; I left no evidence of my theft.

Tonight went as perfectly as it could have. I hadn't anticipated the nurse vomiting, but it's a nice touch and only adds to the thought that everyone is afflicted with a short bug.

Lying on my pillow, I'm tired but feel accomplished.

The little girl puts her head on my chest. "I knew you'd do great."

I stroke her hair. "We're not done yet. I have to make sure Vic knows the files are there."

"That should be the easiest part," Mary chimes in.

She's not wrong. All I have to do now is sit back, point my lopsided smile in the direction of anyone who interacts with me, and wait for Vic.

Thirty-Eight

I wake the next day invigorated.

Hope is a flame that this place nearly managed to snuff out, but I didn't let it. Now it's burning strong. There's less to go wrong now. The hard part is over.

Knowing my files are under the mattress is like having an itch you can't scratch, but I know that I can't safely look at them until quiet time. With everything that has happened, it isn't worth the risk.

At breakfast, I tell Judy 1 that we're getting out of here soon. I know that she won't tell anyone. She probably won't remember by lunch.

"Oh, that's nice," she says.

I wonder what will happen to her when we're all rescued from this place. Does she have family that will take her in? Was the orderly right that she'll find a man to take care of her? I can't stand the thought that she has to rely on someone else because of what they did to her.

Delaney comes to get me after morning rounds, and I sit in her office to draw portraits. She looks tired today. Worn down. Her voice is rough, like she swallowed wool.

"How are you doing today, Nadia?"

I smile at her, lopsided, eyes just slightly crossed. "I'm fine, thank you for asking, Nurse Delaney."

She sighs. "That's good to hear. I'm glad someone is."

I let a frown slowly take over my face. "Is something wrong, Nurse Delaney?"

Realizing her mistake, she softens. "Oh, no, dear. No. Just a long night shift last night. Nothing to worry about."

I brighten. "Oh, okay," I say, then turn to the table to continue drawing.

She leaves, satisfied that I'm still foggy and compliant.

On my way to lunch, I notice many of the nurses yawning and looking unwell.

Mary chuckles. "I guess they didn't figure it out; they're still drinking from the coffeepot."

"That makes sense," I tell her. "The biggest dose would have been the first brew last night, but I would guess there will be a little something extra in the next few brews, too."

Smiling, I take another look around the room. The orderlies don't look any better. None of the staff who worked the night shift last night are around. They must be home, recovering from their unfortunate, sudden illness.

It's hard not to bask in my own glory today. It's so powerful that it dulls the hurt of my husband leaving me. I'm not done grieving, but today is a much-needed reprieve from those feelings. It's a day to celebrate and count our blessings.

We're getting out of here.

After lunch, I'm practically vibrating with excitement. It takes everything in me to hide it from the staff and other patients. More than anything, I want to understand what's been done to me. I want confirmation that my memory loss is not my fault.

The little girl does cartwheels down the hallway to 108. I smile. It's impossible not to feel motherly toward her, even knowing she's just a part of me.

I wait as patiently as possible for the nurse to administer rounds and leave. Once she does, I lie on the bed and bide my time, making sure nobody is coming back.

When I'm sure Judy is asleep, I pull the folder out from under the mattress.

I open the first one, *Moren, Nadia.*

There's the misspelling Vic talked about. I open the file and start with the generic information.

Here's my intake form: *Nadia Moren.* I look closer. The 'e' has been altered from an "a." I look up at Mary and the little girl in shock. Their looks mirror my own.

Somebody did this on purpose. My file was tampered with.

I try to sit with this information for a moment. Who would do that? Who would want to keep me here, and why?

When between the three of us, no explanation comes, I read on. Aside from my name, there's an address (Pebble Drive) and then standard information: height, weight, sex, eye color. There's a blurb from the doctor at my intake.

Patient shows signs of psychosis and aggression. Sedated immediately.

Well, that makes sense. Sedation is their favorite strategy here.

I briefly scan the rest of the document, noting that the intake date is August 4th. I've been here about four and a half months. I don't have any recollection, but that feels right.

The following document lists meds and ECT sessions.

ECT Session performed – August 4th

ECT Session performed – August 7th
ECT Session performed – October 5th
ECT Session performed – November 11th
ECT Session performed – November 28th
ECT Session performed – December 10th

Patient tolerates Thorazine and Lithium with no complications.

Sure, no complications except complete and total loss of my memories. This otherwise sounds right.

Interesting that outside of the first two sessions, they get closer and closer together. I look at the others. They also know what this means.

We're looking at a list of all the times the doctors tried to erase them.

I take a deep breath. I knew this, but I didn't realize how many times we've been through it. It's a miracle that we made it through and pulled everything off.

There's also a list of the times they had to sedate me. I'm surprised by how long it is, but I shouldn't be. I've been fighting for my memories and my life since I got here. I'm lucky to have not ended up on their list for experimental surgery.

Looking at my chart, it's a wonder that I didn't. I've fought back more than I've been complacent.

Given the file's thoroughness, I'm not expecting much from the *Patient Outcomes* file.

Opening the folder, I'm initially surprised at how robust it is.

ECT Session performed
ECT Session performed
ECT Session performed

Subject transferred to Research Unit
Neuro-mapping initiated
Neuro-mapping finished successfully
ECT Session performed
ECT Session performed
ECT Session performed
Amygdalotomy Initiated
Amygdalotomy finished successfully
ECT Session performed
Cingulotomy Initiated
Adverse neurological event noted
Non-responsive to intervention
Cingulotomy discontinued
Primary physician notified
Support withdrawn per protocol
Preservation prep authorized
Time of death: 2:17 am
Transfer to Mortuary completed
Family Notified
Patient File closed

Well, this is thankfully not my file. Looking at the date, it's a decade old.

This poor woman.

My heart lurches.

They've been doing this for a decade? I didn't dig into the *Grants* file, but I hope that it's all listed there.

Looking down, I'm searching for the name of this poor, tortured soul.

Mira Moren – DOB 10/05/1941 DOD 10/31/63

Jesus Christ. She was only twenty-two years old. I glance at Mary and the little girl, but they don't meet my eyes.

"What?"

Mary looks up. "You know."

My blood runs cold, and I start to sweat. "What do I know?"

I can feel the memory pushing against my brain.

But I don't want this one.

Please let it go away.

It doesn't.

It rips through my brain, causing damage that I know I won't be able to undo.

"No, please."

Mary looks at me, eyes full of sorrow. The little girl is openly crying.

"I can't; it hurts too much. Please make it go away."

Mira. My sister.

Thirty-Nine

The memory hits so hard that I can't see. I'm blinded by it.

Mira and I are six and eight years old in our green velvet Christmas dresses and matching bows. Spinning around, faster and faster, as our braids whip around with us. It's a competition now, seeing who can make their dress fly out the farthest. Falling to the floor, dizzy and giggling. Mom is looking on from the couch, smiling.

The board game memory comes back to me, more vivid this time.

Mira is sitting on my right side, eyes wide, unsure how to react to my anger over losing the game. Mom tickles me, and I laugh, but I'm still mad.

Mira leans over and hugs me. "It's okay, Nadia. You still beat me!"

I look down at her with affection. She's so cute, I can't help but let the anger melt away. I hug her back. Everything is okay.

The playground memory expands.

We're on the playground. I scrape my knee at the bottom of the slide. The dark-haired boy takes me over to sit and goes to collect a Band-Aid. Mira is sitting next to me, cross-legged, holding my hand. She puts her head on my shoulder, and though she doesn't speak, she's supporting me. My sister.

The memories come faster now. They're a waterfall. I can't stop them.

She's in junior high. Her blonde hair has turned light brown as she enters her teen years.

I knock on her bedroom door and poke my head in.

She looks up from reading her comic. "What?"

I smile at her. "Just checking in. I haven't seen you in a couple days."

She rolls her eyes. "I've been busy." Even in the awkward throes of puberty, she's beautiful.

I invite myself in and sit on the bed next to her. "Whatcha reading?"

She rolls her eyes again and shows me the cover. "Captain America. Can't you read?" Her voice is soft and teasing, and her green eyes show me she's being playful.

Another memory is coming on, and I don't want it. Please, just leave it be. I can't. Take it back.

Mira is twenty-one years old.

I'm in the visitors' lounge, and she's sitting across the table from me.

"Are you okay?" I ask.

"I'm fine," she replies. But she's not fine. Her hair is limp, cheeks hollow, and her eyes are lifeless. She's a shell of the woman she was.

I'm crying. "Mira, please. Talk to me. What's going on here?" My voice is frantic. "When I get home, I'm going to talk to Mom and Dad. We can't leave you here. I didn't like this idea to begin with, and now I'm certain I was right."

Mira looks up at me and makes eye contact, but there's no spark of recognition. "I'm sorry, who are you?"

No more. Please.

I'm standing at a freshly dug grave. It's November. Cold. The wind attacks me, and I cling tighter to my black jacket. Mom is standing next to me. At her side is a man I don't recognize. He's been crying. Vic is on my other side, hugging me while I sob into his shoulder.

The priest finishes his prayer over the grave, and we each take a flower to place on her casket. The wind whips the roses' scent around, but it's bitter. I bite my lip and taste blood and tears.

"I don't understand," I tell Vic. "I don't know how this happened."

Clipping her green velvet bow to the rose, I place it on the casket.

Vic puts his arm around me, and we turn and walk toward the exit, leaving her behind forever.

"No!" I have to suppress the primal scream that is threatening to come out of my body. My eyes have been squeezed shut, but I open them.

"Why didn't you tell me?"

Mary doesn't meet my eyes. "We didn't know."

I glare at her. "Of course you did. You had to."

The little girl is looking at me. She's not just any little girl. I know every curve of her face, every strand of hair. The sparkle in those green eyes.

"I'm sorry," I tell her through my tears. "I can't look at you. At either of you."

I carefully put the paperwork back in the folder and hide it under my mattress. How am I going to get through today? Or tomorrow? Or any day for the rest of my life?

All I wanted was my memories back.

Now I wonder how I'm going to live with them.

I'm a shell of myself. There's no need to pretend to be foggy and desolate. That's who I am now.

There's still a lot I don't understand, but it doesn't matter anymore. None of it does.

My husband left.

So what? Mira is dead.

I'm insane, and I live in an institution.

So what? Mira is dead.

Is her death what pushed me over the edge? It's the only thing that makes sense. I can't look at the other two, but all paths lead back to her. She's the reason I went crazy. My brain couldn't handle what happened to her, so I came here and let them clear my head.

It was better that way.

I consider not telling Vic about the documents under the table. Maybe I don't want to leave. Maybe I want them to take the pain away again.

Take it forever, even if the cost is my life.

Afternoon activities are a blur. I sit in front of the TV, watching reruns of *I Dream of Jeannie.*

I don't need medication to be numb. My heart might as well have stopped.

There is nothing left.

Give me what Judy 1 had. At least then I can be quietly complacent in what's left of my life.

Nurse Delaney comes over, confused that I'm watching TV and not sketching.

There's no more act. No lopsided smile.

"What's wrong, Nadia?" She sounds like she's underwater.

Is she talking to me? She must be. She used my name. "Oh, what?"

"I asked, What's wrong? You're not sketching."

I look up at her, confused. "Oh. Was I supposed to?"

She looks surprised. "Um, no, you don't have to. Not if you don't want to."

"Okay." I look away, back at the TV.

She moves away quickly, her discomfort apparent, even to my shell.

I don't eat at dinner. Just sit and stare.

A nurse comes by, puts food in my mouth, and tells me to chew.

I do.

She comes back ten minutes later and does it again. This time, she's mad.

"Nadia, you can eat on your own!" She shoves the fork in my mouth, accidentally stabbing my gums.

I taste blood, but it doesn't matter.

She leaves, and I continue staring into space.

Mary tries to get my attention, but I don't look at her. I can't. Every time I do, I see Mira. Being numb is easier than feeling it all.

After dinner, I sit in front of the TV and don't move. I'm not watching it, but it hurts less than sketching, doing a puzzle, or reading a magazine. I only want to be still, to exist the least amount necessary to survive.

Evening rounds come and go, and I lie in bed. Surviving.

Everything hurts. My body. My mind. I'm not sure I still have a soul, but if I do, it hurts.

Suddenly, I feel it. Pushing at my brain.

"No!"

I don't want more memories. I don't even want the ones I have right now.

I look over, and Mary is staring at me, willing me to let it come. She thinks that I need it. That it will give me clarity.

I don't want clarity.

She doesn't know yet, but I'm going to do it.

I reach into the hole in my mattress and pull out the little cup.

Mary's eyes go wide. "No. Nadia… don't."

I smile at her sadly. "Bye, Mary."

The little girl looks up at me from the end of my bed. Her pajamas are dirty. So is her hair. She looks tired. Her eyes lock on mine, but she doesn't plead with me.

Somehow, she understands better than Mary does why I need to do this.

"I'll miss you," I whisper to her.

Then I take two pills.

Forty

I wake up foggy.

Where am I? Oh, right. My room.

Nurse Delaney comes in for morning rounds, and I take my pill. I think they may have given me too much yesterday, but I don't argue.

It's not a good idea to argue.

At breakfast, it's hard to hold the spoon. Or is it a fork?

I pick it up and examine it carefully. It's definitely a spoon. I think.

Judy 1 and Mary sit with me, though Mary doesn't look at anything or talk to anyone. She always stares into space.

The nurses don't bother her like they bother me.

Didn't we use to have another roommate? What was her name… Sandy? No… Betty?

That sounds right. I wonder what happened to her.

One of the nurses comes over to ask me about something to do with portraits, but I don't know what she's talking about. I tell her I'm sorry, but she must have the wrong person.

I think she left, but it's hard to tell. Everything is blurry. Everyone is blurry.

The day slowly slides by in a haze.

Time for meds again. They definitely gave me too much, but I don't complain.

Is it puzzle time?

Looking down at a half-assembled puzzle, it seems familiar. I pick up a piece, and there's a child on a swing. They look happy. That's nice.

Time for lunch already? I'm not hungry, but I'll try.

I stab at something on my tray. It's slimy and slides off the fork. Maybe I don't need lunch.

A nurse comes over and sternly tells me I have to eat.

I almost argue, but then remember that arguing is a bad idea.

Eating a little, I look around. The dining hall seems to shimmer, all the shapes blurring together. Some are people, others are tables or chairs.

It's warm in here, but not unpleasant. Other than the odor, anyway.

After lunch, I shuffle back to my room. I look up. 104. No, that's not it. Shuffle. Look up. 106. Nope, just a little further. Shuffle. Look up. 108. Ah, here it is.

The doctor is already here, working with Judy 1. I can't remember his name, but he has an upside-down heart-shaped birthmark on his cheek that I try not to look at. It seems rude to stare.

He comes over to me next. "Good afternoon, Nadia. How are you feeling today?"

"I'm fine, thank you," I reply. I want to tell him my meds are too strong, but I don't. It's not a good idea to argue.

He mumbles briefly to the nurse, who hands me a paper cup and some water.

I take the pill and lie down to rest.

My eyes open. I don't think anyone came in to wake me up, but I can't be sure. Sitting up, I rub the grit from them. Nope, everything is still blurry. Judy 1 is still sleeping, and Mary is staring into space.

Mary is weird. She makes me uncomfortable, though I'm not sure why.

My fingers feel a weird spot in my mattress. Getting off the bed for a closer look, I see there's a hole that's been safety-pinned together.

I unpin it to see how big it is. Bigger than I would have thought.

What's that?

There's a cup with pills in it. Notes. The nurses' names and schedules, and the address for someone named Nadia Moran. There are also sketches that Nadia must have drawn. She's pretty good.

Huh. Maybe she had this bed before I did.

Wait. Isn't my name Nadia? I think it is. But I didn't do these.

I shove everything back in the mattress and pin it. I don't want to get into trouble.

An orderly flings the door open. "Activity time! Nadia Moren, visitor!"

Why does that name sound familiar? It almost feels like that name is pushing through my brain.

I abandon the thought. Oh well.

I shuffle down the hall to the activity room, following the herd.

The TV's soft, warm glow is like a hug. Comforting and familiar.

A nurse taps my shoulder. "Nadia, you were supposed to go to the visitors' lounge. Your brother is here to see you."

"Oh, sorry. I didn't realize."

I have a brother?

Shuffling down the hall, I keep stopping.

Where am I going again? I look up and see the procedure room. A chill goes down my spine. I don't want to go in there.

I'm standing in the middle of the hall, motionless. Mind blank.

A dark-haired nurse comes over to me. "Nadia, what are you doing?"

I look over at her, but she's blurry. "I… I'm not sure."

She sighs. "You're supposed to be in the visitors' lounge. You have a visitor."

"Oh, right. Thank you." I start to shuffle forward, but within thirty seconds, I've forgotten again where I'm headed.

The nurse comes up beside me and takes my arm, guiding me to the visitors' lounge.

I thank her again and step inside.

It's warm in here. That's nice.

Looking around, all the tables are full. I'm not sure where I'm supposed to be.

A nurse looks up from her book as a man comes over from somewhere out of my line of sight and asks if I'm okay.

"Huh?" I didn't really hear what he said.

"Nadia, are you okay?" He sounds alarmed.

I look up at him. He's handsome. Kind of rugged for my taste, but handsome all the same. "I'm fine, thank you."

He leads me over to a table in the corner that I hadn't been able to see from the doorway.

"Nadia, what's going on?" He sounds terrified. Or angry? I can't tell.

"Nothing, I'm fine." These chairs are soft. Oh, and the stripes are different textures.

"You are *not* fine. What happened?" He's looking at me as if he expects an answer.

I look at him carefully. He looks familiar. Where do I know him from?

"It smells nice in here," I say conversationally.

He throws himself back in his chair. "I can't believe this." Then he leans forward, putting his head in his hands. "I can't believe we're back to this. What did they do to you?"

I was only half paying attention because the underside of the table is cool. It has a strangely smooth, soft feel. I slide my hand across it, unobstructed. "Who?" I ask.

He stares at me, mouth hanging open. Tears form in his eyes, but they don't fall. "This can't happen again, Nadia." He looks down at the table. "This wasn't supposed to happen."

I reach over and put my hand on his. "It's okay. Don't cry. It's okay." I'm not sure why he's upset, but I don't want him to cry.

He looks up at me, wounded. "Do you even remember me right now? Do you remember her? Mira? You can't let what happened to her happen to you. You need to hang on."

Mira. Who is Mira? I squint, trying to remember if I know someone by that name.

I don't know a Mira. But it's a beautiful name.

"Nadia."

I realize I've been staring at the carpet. Looking up at him, I can see the deep sorrow in his eyes.

"Yes?"

"Do you know who I am?"

I don't want to sound callous, but I can't lie to him. "You look familiar, but I don't know you. I'm sorry."

He puts his head in his hands. "I don't know if I'll survive this time. You have to fight it."

Fight what? Oh, his hand is warm. I turn it over and trace the lines on it with my finger. Looking up, I'm startled that he's looking back at me. "What?"

He sighs as if the world is on his back. "You're a fighter, Nadia. This isn't who you are. The last time we talked, you were going to change everything. For everyone here, not just for yourself."

"Me?" That doesn't sound like me. I don't change things. That sounds like arguing. And arguing is a bad idea.

Looking directly into my eyes, he holds my hand. "You, Nadia. You're more than this."

Could I be more than this? Is he right?

The visit is ending. He hugs me tightly and tells me to hold on. To fight, even if I don't think I can.

I walk back out into the hall.

That was weird. I hope he's okay.

At dinner, Mary stares at nothing.

Judy 1 asks how my visit was.

"What visit?" Did I have a visitor?

She smiles politely, then turns back to her tray.

Afterwards, I stare at the TV for a while. The glow is comforting.

A nurse asks me something about portraits, but she must be thinking of someone else. I can't even draw stick figures.

During evening rounds, I think maybe I should tell the nurse that my meds are too strong, but I don't.

In the darkest part of the night, I wake briefly. What was that noise?

I look over, and Judy 1 is asleep.

Mary is sitting up, listening. "Did you hear that?"

Her voice is oddly familiar.

A wave of nausea rips through me. "Hear what?"

She looks in my direction, making eye contact. "The screams."

"No. I didn't hear anything." Lying back down, I fall right back to sleep.

My eyes open. I'm foggy. Wiping the grit, I open them again. Nope, still foggy. Maybe I should tell the nurse my meds are too strong? No. That's a bad idea. I shouldn't argue.

Judy 1 is sitting on the edge of her bed as the nurse administers meds.

I wait complacently for mine, then take them with water.

At breakfast, I'm not hungry.

A nurse comes by and shoves some food in my mouth. Some of it spills back onto the tray as I try to chew.

There's a commotion a few tables over. By the time I focus my eyes, it's over. Two orderlies are dragging a limp woman away.

I shudder. This is why we don't argue.

A nurse who looks familiar—maybe the one who asked about portraits—walks by and slows, but ultimately keeps going.

At OT, we have craft supplies. I make a Christmas wreath out of pipe cleaners. I'm half-finished when it's over, but they say we can continue working tomorrow. I'm glad. This was fun.

Lunchtime creeps up on me. I sit at my table with Judy 1 and Mary. Why does my brain call her Judy 1 when she's the only Judy? Probably because I'm crazy. That makes sense.

Judy 1… I mean, Judy quietly eats her lunch. She's pretty. Her hair is a mess, though. I want to reach out and touch it, to see if it feels as rough as it looks. I start to reach, but a nurse comes by and tells me to eat.

Didn't I eat? I thought I had. Looking down, my tray is full. Hmm. Picking up my fork, I try to spear a piece of meat, but it slides off. I fight with it for a minute, then raise it to my mouth. I can't close it fast enough, and it falls out. I let out a sigh, frustrated.

A nurse, maybe the same one, comes by and shoves the meat into my mouth. I chew obediently.

Shuffling back to my room, I look up. There's a song playing on the radio in the nurses' station. The tune sounds familiar, but my brain doesn't process the words. They come too fast, and then I'm past the station and back at 108.

A doctor is in my room. He chides me for taking too long to get back after lunch. I apologize quietly. Don't argue.

When he leaves, I curl up on my bed. Everything is foggy. I'm tired.

I'm just drifting off to sleep when I hear a loud noise. It sounds like shouting from the hall.

Forty-One

Someone probably argued. I lie in bed, waiting for the orderlies to take care of it. The shouting doesn't stop. I hear the sound of heavy footsteps and men barking orders. A woman screams.

My door bursts open, and men in combat boots and tactical gear push through it. "Get up! Everyone! Out in the hall!"

My heart rate skyrockets. What's going on?

The men are blurry, but they don't leave. "GET UP!"

I shakily get out of bed. Did I argue? I don't remember arguing. I put my slippers on and shuffle out into the hall.

The hallway is a madhouse. Ha. It's not funny, though.

The blurry men are everywhere, herding people out to the dining hall. One screams at me, "Get going!"

I shuffle as fast as I can in line with all the others. What is going on?

The dining hall fills with scared patients. Everyone is shaking. I'm sweating. Briefly, I sit at my table, but a man grabs me and takes me to a corner of the hall.

"Nadia, are you okay?" He has dark hair. He's handsome, in a rugged way. Is he familiar? Maybe. Do I know him?

"I… What's happening?" I'm scared and foggy, and the lights are too bright. I'm supposed to be napping. Why am I in the dining hall? Did I do something wrong?

The sound of heavy boots, women screaming, and patients crying is overwhelming, and I sink to the floor and curl into a ball. I put my head in my hands. My brain is trying to wrap itself around what's happening, but it can't. This room smells like fear. Like sweat, urine, and hopelessness.

The man gently stands me back up and hugs me.

I sink into his chest. I want to cry, but I can't. I'm too numb, and my body won't allow it.

He yells to someone. "Hey! I want a stretcher over here, now!" He continues holding me.

Despite the craziness going on around me, I momentarily feel safe.

Two men with a stretcher come over, and the hugging man helps me onto it.

"I'll be by in a few hours to check on you. Just focus on getting better, okay? Everything is over; you don't have to worry anymore. We did it, Nadia." He places his hand on my cheek briefly and looks into my eyes. He stands for a moment and watches as I'm transported outside to a waiting ambulance.

The ambulance is quiet. They don't turn on the siren.

The attendants are nice. I'm handed water and given a warm blanket. They tell me I can sit if I want, but I lie down anyway.

I wake up confused. Someone is gently telling me to stand up and helping me down some steps.

It's cold. Are we outside?

A nurse is waiting with a wheelchair. She's smiling. "You feeling okay, hon?"

"I… I think so." I'm not sure where I am or what's happening, but I sit.

She wheels me into the hospital, past a desk, and over to a set of elevators. A phone rings, and it echoes in my head. It's too loud. The lights are too bright.

The nurse presses a button, and now we're moving up. "It's cold out there today, huh?" She's trying to make conversation.

"Yes, I'm cold." I am cold. I'm freezing.

She wheels me out of the elevator and down a hallway. It smells of disinfectant, but something is off. It smells clean. Not harsh.

It's a much smaller hallway than I'm used to seeing. What part of the institute are we in?

"Oh, poor dear. We'll get you situated in your room, and I'll bring you some extra blankets and some tea. Does that sound good?" Her voice is kind. It sounds strange in my ears.

"Tea?" Does Ravensbrook have tea?

"Would you prefer coffee?" She wheels me into a room with two bays, curtained off for privacy. We go to the second one. It has a window with a view of the parking lot.

I look over at the other bay. It's empty. "N-no. Tea sounds wonderful, thank you."

Why does this feel like a trick?

"Okay, let's get you into bed."

The bed is larger and more comfortable than what I'm used to. There's a call button by the pillow. A sink is on the opposite wall. The radiator by the window hisses as it releases heat.

She helps me into bed. "Did you want to sit up, or lie down, hon?"

Am I allowed to make choices? Do we have choices here? "Whatever is easier," I tell her. I don't want to get in trouble.

"Well," she says. "If I'm going to bring you some tea, you should probably sit up." She goes to the foot of the bed and cranks it until I'm in a sitting position. "I'll be back in a few minutes with tea, and we need to start an IV. To make sure you're hydrated, for now."

"Oh… okay. Thank you."

She departs, and I look out the window. It's clean, and I can see a bird in a tree just to the right.

It's disorienting. Why is the window clean?

I'm nervous.

What is happening? Where am I?

A few minutes later, I startle as the nurse comes back in with a cup of tea.

"Here you go, hon. Have a few sips, and then I need to get that IV started." She walks over to the cart and grabs a glass bottle, hanging it from the IV hook.

The tea is warm and comforting, even though my hand shakes as I hold it. It soothes my frayed nerves in a way my meds haven't.

The nurse starts my IV, and it's done quickly. She looks satisfied with her job well done.

My tea is gone, and I'm sleepy. "Could… Would you mind… just putting the bed down so I can sleep?"

"Oh, of course. No problem at all." She cranks the bed back down flat so I can rest. As she's leaving the room, she turns back around. "I forgot to tell you, if you need something, just hit that call button, and I'll be right along, okay?"

I turn my head to the left and look at the call button. "Okay, thank you."

I'm warm and comfortable. The tea was like a hug on the inside that I really needed.

Closing my eyes, I hear the clock on the wall ticking the seconds away.

The hum of the radiator soothes me, and I drift off to sleep.

Forty-Two

I'm woken some time later by the nurse. A doctor is standing at the foot of the bed, looking at my chart.

"How are you feeling, Nadia?" He looks kind, and his voice is deep, but soft.

"I… Where am I?" I don't recognize the room I'm in. Where are my roommates?

He sets the chart down on the bed and sits next to me. "You're at Saint Joseph's Hospital. You came from Ravensbrook, a psychiatric institute about an hour away. Do you remember any of that?"

I close my eyes and think. Ravensbrook, yes. I remember that. "I remember Ravensbrook," I tell him.

He nods. "Good. I'm glad we have a baseline to start with." He picks up the clipboard with my chart. "You don't remember the ambulance ride?"

I close my eyes again. I hear shouting and heavy boots on the ground. I feel a firm hug. Someone is handing me a blanket. But that's all.

"No," I tell him. "I'm sorry." I hang my head. I hope they're not upset with me.

"It's okay. Nothing to be sorry about." He stands up and turns to the nurse. "I'm putting her on a light dose of benztropine. Discontinue the Thorazine. I want to get her to the point where she's lucid, and then we'll get a new baseline."

The nurse nods and hurries away to carry out his orders.

The doctor turns back to me. "We're going to get you fixed up, and when you're feeling better, we'll send you home."

"Home?" I'm confused. Ravensbrook is my home. It's where I live. "You mean Ravensbrook?" Where else would I go?

He shakes his head sadly. "No, Ravensbrook has been shut down. You have family who will take you home as soon as you're well enough. They should be here soon to visit." He moves toward the door. "It's going to be okay, Nadia. You're in good hands here." The door shuts quietly behind him.

I'm so confused, and still more than a little scared. What happened at Ravensbrook? Why is it shut down? I have family? My chest tightens uncomfortably.

I'm unsure why.

The nurse hustles back in with a pill for me to take. I take it with water and open my mouth so she can check.

She laughs, but it sounds sad. "You don't need to do that here, hon. You're safe now."

The words sound foreign, and I'm still confused.

I fall into a restless sleep as the new pill works its way through my system.

The next time I wake, my mind is less foggy.

I open my eyes. It's late in the day, and the light streams through the window. The sun is setting over the trees on the other side of the parking lot.

That's right, the hospital. I'm in the hospital.

My hand shakes as I reach for a cup of water that's been left for me on my tray. Taking a sip, I look to the other side of the room and almost spill it on myself.

A man is sitting on my other side. He's got dark hair. He's handsome. Rugged, like an action movie hero. He looks exhausted. "Hi." He smiles at me.

Putting my water down, I try to find my voice. "H-hello."

His face falls. "You still don't know me, do you?"

"I'm so sorry. Should I?" He looks devastated, and I wish I could make it better, but I don't want to lie to him. The guilt rises within me.

"The doctor says it will take time, but that your memories will come back." He takes my hand, holding it gently.

My memories? Come to think of it, I don't remember much from before today. I have a vague recollection of living at Ravensbrook, but no clear memories of it.

"How long will it take?" I ask him, shifting uncomfortably in the bed.

Getting up, he goes over to the crank and lifts the head of the bed until I'm comfortable. "They said it could be hours or days. But once the Thorazine is fully out of your system, your memory will come back."

I settle back into my pillow, relaxing. I'm comfortable with him, though I don't know why. My body knows he's safe, even if my mind doesn't yet. "What do we do until then?"

He smiles. "I'm not going anywhere until you've recovered. You've been in that institution for nearly five months. They've been the hardest months of my life."

He's sweet, and he obviously cares about me. I don't think it's romantic; that's not the feeling I get.

"Can you tell me about my life? Maybe if you fill me in, the memories will come back faster?" It's sound logic, to me at least.

He darkens. "The doctor says I shouldn't. He wants your brain to do the work itself. So you can recover as much as possible."

"As much as possible? Is there a chance I won't recover?" This is alarming. What if I'm stuck with amnesia for the rest of my life? How bad is it if he can't tell me? I tighten my grip on the blanket.

He turns his face away from me, as if he can't bear to look at me as he delivers the news. "There is a chance, but it's small." Looking back at me, he insists, "But that isn't going to happen. I won't let it."

I smile at him. He's someone who is used to getting his way. I hope this time it goes in his favor. In both of our favors.

I'm tired now. Even this short visit is emotionally exhausting. "I'm sorry, but is it all right if I sleep? I'm so tired." I look at him shyly, only slightly worried that he'll be mad.

"Of course it's all right!" He cranks my bed back down so that I can rest. "I'll be in the waiting area. The nurse can let me know when you're awake again."

I breathe a sigh of relief. He isn't mad. I can trust him. Of course I can. Why does my chest hurt?

As he's leaving, he stops, then turns to look at me. "Nadia, we're going to get through this. You're going to be okay." And then he's gone.

I lie back on the pillow, my mind racing. The radiator hums. It feels safe, but still wrong.

I'm scared.

What happens now?

I close my eyes, and I'm asleep.

When I wake again, it's dark. There's a small light on a switch near the bed. I click it on.

I need to pee. Badly.

I hit the call button. Instinctively, I worry that the nurse won't come. Or she's so busy she won't make it in time.

My body braces for the long haul. I need to hold it.

The nurse pops her head in. "Everything okay?"

Wow. That was really quick. "Um, yes, I'm fine. I… need to … relieve myself." I flinch, waiting for an eye roll or a heavy sigh to show that I'm bothering her.

"Oh, no problem, hon." She walks in, lowers the bed, and helps me up. "Can you walk?"

I'm shocked. "Yes, I can. Thank you."

She takes my arm until I'm steady and then walks me out into the hall, then a few doors down. "Do you need help, or can you manage? I can come in with you or wait out here; it's totally up to you."

"I can manage, thank you so much." I step into the bathroom. I don't know why, but I'm crying.

"Oh, I forgot to tell you, don't lock the door. If you feel faint, I need to be able to get to you quickly." She raises her voice so I can hear her through the door.

"Okay!" I yell back. I relieve myself, then stand back up to flush and wash my hands. I'm sobbing. Why am I sobbing?

The nurse opens the door. "Are you okay? I heard crying." She rushes over. "Are you hurt? What's wrong?"

I hiccup through the sobs. "I don't know… I'm not sure."

She looks at me sadly. "Nadia, let's get you back to bed. It's okay. You're okay." She takes my arm and walks with me back to my room and tucks me into bed. "Get some more rest. Your vitals are great, and I won't bug you again until the morning when the doctor wants to reexamine you."

She leaves, and her friendliness and concern make me cry harder.

What happened to me? Am I broken?

I lie back down, but sleep doesn't come.

Forty-Three

There's a chair in the corner. A little blonde girl is sitting on it.

I start, then look around. Did I get a roommate? No, I'm still the only one here.

She makes eye contact, and I ask gently, "Are you okay? Are you lost?"

She hugs her knees to her chest. "No, I'm not lost." Her eyes are sad, cheeks tear-stained. She rocks slightly. "I'm here to remind you. You know that."

Remind me? "Of what, honey?" I'm confused. My breath comes in small gasps, but I don't understand why.

She gets down from the chair. Her pajamas are torn and stained. Walking slowly, she shuffles over to my bed and gently takes my hand, opening it palm up.

I look at her, still confused.

In my palm, she places a red rose with a green velvet bow clipped to it. As she looks into my eyes, her tears form again.

I drop the rose, hands shaking. I feel as if I've been struck by lightning. The memories flood into my head, a tidal wave of fear, sadness, anger, happiness, and regret, all bundled together.

Wrapped tightly, a gift I never wanted. I close my eyes and let out a low howl as my brain tries to reject it.

Mira. Vic. Mom and Dad. Ravensbrook. ECT. The humiliation. Inedible food. The institutional cruelty.

I remember all of it.

I didn't want to remember, but here I am.

Sobbing, I hit the call button. A moment later, a nurse pops her head in. "You okay, hon? What do you need?"

Through my sobs, I get out, "Is… *sob*… Vic… *sob*… still… *sob*… in the waiting… *sob*… room?" I need him. Now.

She nods at me, then says kindly, "I'll grab him for you, dear. Just hang on." Then she disappears.

I look around for the little girl, but she's gone.

Almost as if she never existed.

The door flies open, and Vic comes running into the room. "Nadia! Are you okay?" He looks half asleep, as if the nurse had just woken him.

Sobbing, I get out of bed. "Vic, I remember. I remember Mira." The wail that comes out of me is barely human. It's the sound of sorrow so profound that the mind can't fully comprehend the loss.

He rushes over and puts his arms around me, and I cry large, wet tears onto his shirt. Vic stays quiet, letting me have this moment of loss all over again.

Finally, as my tears slow and my sobbing becomes softer, he speaks. "I'm so sorry, Nadia. I miss her too, every day."

I sniffle, still hugging him. "I don't remember everything, but I remember her. I remember Ravensbrook, I remember how scary it was putting the files under the table." I look at him as realization hits. "How did you find them? Have we had a visit since I put them there? Did I tell you? There's a lot from when I was medicated that I don't remember."

Somehow, this shatters him more. "Yes, we had a visit. No, you didn't tell me. I found them anyway. We planned this months ago. You followed it, even without your memories."

I look at him, confused. "Months ago?"

"You still don't remember." He looks sad.

"I remember a lot, even some things from before the institution. But not everything." I sit down hard on the bed. "After remembering Mira, I couldn't take it. I dosed myself because the memories were trying to surface, and I couldn't handle more. I was on the precipice of the whole truth, and I needed to be numb. That was after I left the files for you. I found hers…" The tears come again, unrestrained. "I couldn't handle remembering that she died, and that I was so broken that I followed in her footsteps."

Now he looks angry. "What do you mean, followed in her footsteps?"

As I'm about to explain my mental illness to Vic, the door opens, and two more people walk in.

My parents.

Mom rushes over to me and hugs me, tears pouring down her face. "Oh my God, Nadia. I'm so glad you're okay. That you made it out. I spent the last five months without a wink of sleep. But you did it." She breaks down, sobbing into my shoulder.

My confusion spikes. I look behind Vic, at Dad. He's hanging back, unsure how to insert himself into this scenario.

I feel pressure in my head. Sitting down, I close my eyes and tell them, "I feel woozy." The room spins, and the pressure in my head is now pain, sharp and exact, poking through into my skull.

Opening my eyes, my vision blurs, but not from medication. I can feel everything swimming through my head again, ready to surface.

All I have to do is let it.

I lie down and let the room spin. I can't see Vic, but I can hear his concern.

"Nadia, what's happening? Are you okay?"

My head aches, but not nearly as much as my heart does. Suddenly, it's all there. It starts like a scratched record, skipping beats, until it finally settles. The pain in my head is gone.

All that's left are the memories.

I look at Vic, weary but triumphant. "We did it. We really fucking did it."

Craning my neck to see past him, I look at Hank.

"You're a bad actor, but you did it too. Thanks, Chief."

Forty-Four

Hank steps over, looking relieved. "I'm glad not to have to pretend to be your dad anymore. You're right. I'm a terrible actor." He smiles at me wearily.

The last few months have taken a toll on all of us.

"Vic," I say through my tears, "You held all of this together. I don't know if I can ever tell you how grateful I am. I wouldn't have gotten out alive without you."

He weeps openly.

I don't think I've ever seen him cry before. He's one of the toughest agents I've ever met. I feel like I've known him my whole life, because I have.

"Remember the time we were kids, and I fell off the slide at the playground? You've been taking care of me for as long as I can remember. You played the role of big brother like a natural, because you're my brother in every way that matters." I let the memory wash over me again, this time smiling through the tears, through the thought of Mira sitting next to me.

I want to know the rest, the parts I wasn't privy to, right now. "What happened with Ravensbrook? Are they going down?"

Vic smiles at me, wiping away a tear. "They're done. Doors shuttered, doctors arrested, medical companies sued into obscurity. None of them will ever work in the industry again, if they ever get out of jail." He kneels next to the bed, suddenly serious. "None of this was possible without your sacrifice. I can't even begin to imagine the horrors you went through in that place, but you were the only one who could have survived it."

I smile at him sadly. "You know why I needed to do it. After what they did to Mira, I spent a decade trying to figure out how to prove it. I wasn't going to miss that chance, no matter the risk."

I look over at Mom. "I'm so sorry, Mom. For everything. For you, thinking you were going to lose another daughter to that place."

She clears her throat, but tears still well in her eyes. "You avenged her, Nadia. Brought closure that would have never been possible otherwise. I wish your dad were around to see it. He never forgave himself."

"I do too, Mom." Dad died about five years ago. He always blamed himself for what happened to Mira. He's the one who insisted she go to Ravensbrook to cure her unrelenting feminism.

There was nothing wrong with her; he just didn't understand.

The drinking started right after she died.

"I still wonder what she would be like today if she'd gotten the chance to grow up," Mom sobs into a tissue.

I hug her and let her grieve. "She would have been amazing. She *was* amazing."

My heart still hurts for the sister I lost, but finally understanding the whole context, having my memories back, lets me put it all in perspective.

I, Detective Nadia Moran, went to hell and came out the other side. For Mira. For my sister, and everyone like her who was stuck in that fucking pit of an institution.

Something occurs to me, and I look sharply at Vic. "Barbara?"

He sighs and runs his fingers through his hair. "She got away, Nadia. She ran."

Barbara Cross was on the inside with me. She was supposed to protect me. Her job was to go in as Marlene

Delaney, a cheerful RN who would help me by skipping my meds and lowering the ECT dose, if God forbid it got that far. Instead, she used me and tried to silence me, to pull me under. She would have killed me if given the chance.

"She turned, I take it?" My anger simmers just under the surface. My own understatement isn't lost on me.

He snorts. "She more than turned, Nadia. It's like they converted her into a true believer. She thought what they were doing there was valid. She skipped town. We'll try, but we won't find her. Cowards like her always know when to run."

It's a bitter pill to swallow, but we still achieved our goal, even with her actively working against me.

We did it.

For Mira. Always for her.

Forty-Five

I'm sitting on the bed the next day, waiting for the nurse to finish my discharge paperwork so Vic can take me home. He brought me the files and all my notes that were stuffed inside the mattress at Ravensbrook.

Looking fondly at the drawing of Mira at six years old, I can't help but smile through the tears. I loved her so. She was angelic in the way that little girls are, but such a firecracker. I managed to capture her exactly as I always think of her, in her green velvet Christmas dress. She loved it so much she wore it until the velvet wore out, and she outgrew it.

I'm grateful that I was a sketch artist before I became a detective. Having the sketches at Ravensbrook helped me clear the hurdle of my memories so many times. More times than I even know, I'm sure.

I pull out the sketch of my husband. The sadness caused by his leaving is dulled now that I have all of my memories back.

He didn't leave because I was insane. He left because he couldn't handle me avenging my sister, knowing there was a possibility I wouldn't make it out.

I made my choice.

Last, the sketch of 'Mary.' Mira at twenty-two. She was so beautiful and bright. She would have changed the world if she hadn't been murdered. I grimace at the irony that "science" is what killed her.

My heart aches, but I know now that I've done everything I possibly could. Ravensbrook is gone, the scientists and CEOs at Horizon Biomedical are under investigation, and I do not doubt that there are records somewhere of all the other psychiatric hospital populations they've been experimenting on.

I hope every one of them gets what they deserve.

Putting the documents down, I sigh and look at the clock. Vic should be here soon. Where is that paperwork?

I think about Barbara. She's not someone I ever thought would have turned on me. We were only work colleagues, but she was an upstanding and trustworthy officer. How did they get to her? What could they possibly have offered her that was worth her soul?

The nurse steps into the room to go over my discharge papers. I've been cleared to return home.

Home. My little yellow house on Pebble Drive, with periwinkle shutters. Right at the water's edge, where I've always done my best thinking. The hours I've spent sitting in my chair, watching the waves, thinking about Mira, are endless.

"Are you okay, hon? You zoned out there for a minute." She looks worried.

"Oh, no. I'm okay." I smile. "Just thinking about home. I can't wait to sit on my couch." I give a quick laugh.

She smiles at me and continues going over my treatment plan.

I wince at the term.

Vic walks in. He looks rested, like he's finally had a whole night of sleep.

I did too. It's the best sleep I've had in months.

He smiles and waits for the nurse to finish giving instructions.

She hands me the paperwork. "You're all set!" She moves to leave, then turns back. Smiling shyly, she adds, "Thank you for what you did. I worked at a facility like that for a short time right out of school, and it was awful. Nobody deserves that kind of treatment."

I'm choked up. I nod at her and can't form words.

Vic puts his arm around me. "What do you think, kid? Ready to get out of here?"

I smile up at him. "More than you could ever imagine."

Epilogue

I wave to Mrs. Sanderson from across the aisle at the supermarket. "How are you?"

"I'm doing well, dear, how are you?" She smiles over her glasses, her purse hanging at her side.

"I'm great, Mrs. Sanderson, thanks for asking. Say hi to little Bill for me!"

She's a neighbor of mine whom I've known for decades. Her grandson is a good kid and very sweet.

"I will, Nadia. Have a nice day!" She turns and walks over to the frozen foods.

I take my cart to the long checkout line. It's fine, I have nothing else going on today.

It's been about six months since Ravensbrook shut down. The worst perpetrators are all in jail. Doctor Herbert and any staff who assisted him in performing the illegal surgeries will be put away for a long time, and more importantly, will never work in the field again. They've lost their credibility and have been ordered to repay any funds associated with the gruesome activities.

Vic and I helped Betty reunite with her husband and little boy. There was nothing wrong with her to begin with, and she more than did her time.

Judy 1 went home with family. They were happy to take her back now that she's 'cured.'

Four other asylums were incriminated and subsequently shut down when the FBI raided the main offices of Horizon Biomedical. Most of their board and many employees are awaiting trial on multiple charges, from forced medical experimentation and false imprisonment to negligent homicide, racketeering, and federal civil-rights violations.

Vic and Hank are pretty much the same.

Hank did get the key to the city and a Governor's Medal of Honor, and I had to help him write a speech for it. He bumbled it slightly, but in the photo that was in the paper, he looks happy and proud. Deservedly.

Vic and his girlfriend broke up, but I think he's okay. He's married to his job, just like me. We were both promoted to Detective Sergeant, though I'm still out on leave.

We haven't heard anything about Barbara. She disappeared without a trace. We probably won't ever find her, but I've accepted that. We achieved what we wanted to, even with her working against us, and there's something to be said for that.

I've been cleared to go back to light duty as of next week, thanks to months of counseling and continuously improving psych evals. I can't say I'm the same as I was before. I don't think that's really possible. But I've come a long way, and I feel more whole than I have in a very long time.

"Ma'am? Are you all set?" The checkout clerk is staring at me.

"Oh, yes, sorry." I hadn't realized the line had moved so quickly. I hurry to put my items on the conveyor belt and check out.

Carrying my paper bag out to the car, I unlock the trunk and put my groceries inside. It's a beautiful early summer day, and the breeze rustles in the trees. As I close the trunk, it gently gusts through my hair, lifting it off my shoulders. Getting into the car, the seat is hot but pleasant. I roll down my window and put my arm out as I take a left and drive toward home.

I turn on the radio, and *Hotel California* is playing.

I change the station. That song gives me the creeps since being at Ravensbrook. Something about being stuck in a place you can't leave sends a chill up my spine.

The sun on my face and arm feels fantastic, and I lower my sunglasses to keep the glare out of my eyes.

Pulling up to my house on Pebble Drive, I shut the car off and take a minute to admire my home. It's not big, but it's mine, and inside I'm safe. Even from the front of the house, I can hear the waves lapping at the stones that line the oceanfront.

Smiling, I get out and take the groceries out of the trunk. I let myself in the front door and take a deep breath. It smells like home. Like leather, vanilla, and lavender.

I set the groceries on the floor for a moment and pick up the framed photo on the entryway table just by the door.

It's Christmas. I'm eight, and Mira is six. We're in our green velvet dresses, hugging each other, smiling for the photo. It makes me smile. I'll always miss her, but I won't let what happened to either of us sour the incredible life we had as sisters.

Picking the bag back up, I take it to the kitchen and start to put away the groceries. I put the last can of chili into the cupboard, then move to the sink to wash my coffee cup from this morning.

With my chores done, I go into the living room and sink onto my couch. The smell of leather and vanilla is most potent in this room, and it's my favorite.

I close my eyes for a moment. Sensing movement, I open them and look around. I shut them again. "Oh, hi, Mary."

Mary comes over and sits next to me on the couch. "How was the market?"

I yawn. "It was fine. I want to rest, if you don't mind."

The little girl runs across the room in her green dress, chasing a ball. She looks up at me and smiles, then continues playing.

There are some parts of me that Ravensbrook broke that will never fully heal.

But to be honest? I don't mind living with the ghosts of my past.

They are my sister, after all.

Acknowledgements

Writing, for me, makes hours fall away in seconds. It's like reading, but a choose-your-own-adventure book where the characters do what you ask of them, and you control the weather.

It's a feeling that doesn't quite exist in the real world. In truth, it truly takes a community, my chosen family, to allow me the time and space to write.

It's something I am forever grateful for.

To Marc, for wrangling up the kids and taking them to our friend's house to give me a few hours of quiet.

To Jenny and Bob, and Kara and Justin, for opening your homes and giving my kids places where they're comfortable and loved.

Thank you to my beta readers for the invaluable feedback that helped shape the book's ending.

A huge thank you to Hanna Elizabeth, my editor, who made me both laugh and cry with her kind words, especially these: *Keep writing.* The changes you made were subtle but very much needed.

Another shout-out to Clint, my cover artist, who gave this story a face far better than I could have come up with on my own. Your work is magic.

Lastly, to Ryder, Maverick, and Raven, for being amazing, stubborn, beautiful, headstrong, and caring. Never try to change who you are.

Because of you, I found my voice.

About the Author

Nicole Palermo is a New England-based writer of psychological fiction exploring memory and identity. She is the author of *I Haven't Been Myself.*

More at NicolePalermoAuthor.com

Coming Soon from Nicole Palermo

Dark Fragments

Vera has always lived her life carefree. A little wild.

Until the day she wakes up in a hospital bed and everything changes.
Now her memory is unreliable, and she isn't sure who she can trust. When the police require her to try to recover what happened the day her life unraveled, Vera is forced to confront the person she used to be… and the person she's trying to become.

Some fragments were never meant
to be remembered

Coming August 2026

Sneak Peek of
Dark Fragments

One

"I'll tell you everything I remember. It isn't much."

"Let's start with your name and occupation."

I glare at her, irritated. She knows my name. She has all my information. This feels condescending just for the sake of it.

She looks at me evenly, expectantly. Sitting, awaiting an answer, stylus in hand.

I never cared for therapy. I tried it out in college, but it didn't make me feel better. It was just me repeating my problems, being forced to think about them for the sake of 'getting them off my chest.' It never got them off my chest; it caused me to live in an endless loop of frustration.

In the years since, I've forged my own path for moving on.

Grace is already leaving an unpleasant taste in my mouth.

I cross my arms and set my jaw. "Vera Marlowe. Journalist, New York Oracle." Yes, I know my tone is clipped. I'd rather be anywhere else.

I can deal with this on my own terms.

"Good to meet you, Vera," Grace says with a smile. She's sitting in a high-backed executive chair behind a beautiful mahogany desk, and the room smells of leather and expensive perfume. She must be paid handsomely to have an office like this in New York City. It's on the tenth story of a high-rise building, and the lobby is all glass and marble floors. It must cost a fortune to rent.

I shoot her another irritated glance, but don't reply.

She looks to be mid-thirties, but she's 'rich pretty.' You know the type. The women who, if you took away all their expensive clothes, cosmetic procedures, and skin care, and threw them in a trailer park, wouldn't get a second glance. She's got dark hair, a heart-shaped face, and lips perfected by filler. Her eyes are surrounded by makeup done just so, and designer glasses mirror them.

When my reply isn't forthcoming, she tries again. "So, why are you here today, Vera?" She smiles warmly as if we're just two friends having a fireside chat.

"You know why I'm here. You have all my background information and the documentation the doctor sent over. Why are we playing games?" My fists clench. Now I'm not just irritated, I'm angry.

Grace stays even-headed, and I get the feeling it would take a lot to rattle her. "I do know why you're here, but I think it makes sense to hear it directly from you. You don't want others telling your story, do you?" She's still smiling, waiting for me to begin.

"Ugh. This is so stupid." I can't even pretend like I want to do this, never mind the fact that I have no idea how I'm going to do this. I throw my arms up, exasperated, and then fall silent again.

Grace puts down her pen and takes off her expensive glasses. They hang off her crossed fingers. "Vera, I know this is difficult," she says gently, as if she's talking to an obstinate child. "But we have to start somewhere." She presses the tips of her fingers to her lips and continues waiting.

It's quiet for a moment.

Why does this feel like the emotional equivalent of smoking me out of a room?

I hate to let her win, but I also know there is no getting out of this. Legally, I'm required to be here, so I may well get it over with.

I sigh, letting her know one last time how pointless I feel her role here is.

She's still not fazed.

"How far should I go back?" I ask, sarcastically. "28 years ago, my parents fucked. Should we start there?"

Her smile tightens, and I sit back in the chair, appeased that I may have gotten to her.

"Maybe not back that far. Why don't you start with what happened last week?" She puts her glasses back on and looks down at her tablet.

Frowning, I realize I didn't zing her as well as I thought.

Rolling my eyes, I pacify her with what I remember. "I was having a typical week. Hunting for a good story, trying to scrape together rent money so I don't get evicted, and lunch with a friend. Then there's nothing. The last thing I remember is going to bed for the night, and then I woke up in the hospital. Nothing in between. I'm missing roughly a full day."

Grace nods and makes a note on her tablet.

I don't know what she's writing down; she already knows all this.

With a healthy amount of cynicism, I ask, "Am I fixed now, doc? Can I go?"

She looks up, smiling patiently at me. "I think you've got a little more effort to put in today."

Sighing, I stand up. "You know I don't want to be here at all." Walking behind the chair, I turn around and grip the back of it, staring at her.

She nods and looks up from her notes. "I've gotten that hint, yes. You aren't exactly shy about how you're feeling, which is actually a good thing. We just need to redirect your effort."

Pausing, she makes another note in her tablet. Without looking up, she adds, "You aren't going to rattle me, Vera. I'm very good at what I do, and I know I can help you."

Cathy, the social worker assigned to my case, was ecstatic that I got in with Dr. Grace Harrison. She is a highly qualified specialist in therapeutic memory recovery.

I'm required to see her in an attempt to find out why I woke up in the hospital with the shit beaten out of me. It doesn't matter that I don't want to be here.

Falling back into the chair again, I realize that since I don't have a choice, I may as well get it over with. "If I do what you say, will I get my memory back?"

Grace nods again. "Yes. Obviously, nothing is guaranteed, but I'm very optimistic."

"What if I don't want it back?"

www.ingramcontent.com/pod-product-compliance
Lightning Source LLC
LaVergne TN
LVHW091256150826
845673LV00006B/1443

* 9 7 9 8 9 9 4 6 7 0 8 1 1 *